ESPECIALLY FOR GIRLS™ Presents

Allegro Born...
Allegro Dead

by Barbara Corcoran

Originally published as *You're Allegro Dead*

Atheneum   *New York*

This book is a presentation of **Especially for Girls,**™
Weekly Reader Books. Weekly Reader Books offers
book clubs for children from preschool through high school.
For further information write to: **Weekly Reader Books,**
4343 Equity Drive, Columbus, Ohio 43228.

Published by arrangement with
Atheneum Publishers, Inc., A Division of Macmillan, Inc.
Especially for Girls and Weekly Reader
are trademarks of Field Publications.
Printed in the United States of America.

Library of Congress Cataloging in Publication Data

Corcoran, Barbara
  You're allegro dead.
  SUMMARY: Two girls get themselves into deep trouble before they
solve the mystery of who is creating the disturbances at their recently
reopened summer camp.
  [I. Mystery and detective stories] I. Title.
PZ7.C814Yo   [FIC]   81-1906
ISBN 0-689-30840-X   AACR2

TO

Mar, Brack, Frankie, Charlotte, and all the rest.
And good night, Colonel, wherever you are.

Allegro Born . . .
Allegro Dead

1

"Oh, no," Kim said, "not again!" She swung an imaginary tennis racquet and went up on her toes for the serve.

"I know," Stella said. "It's embarrassing. But what can you do?" She sat on the edge of her bed watching Kim.

"I thought reunions took place every five years, or ten, or fifty, not every darned year."

"It just seems like every year. Mom and her camp chums reune when enough of them happen to be within reach of each other. Like last year, when Mrs. Owens was on her way to Europe and stopped off here, and this year when Miss Davenport had this brainstorm."

"What brainstorm?" Kim faced Stella's full-length mirror and did a slow-motion backhand. "My backhand stinks." She was a tall, slender twelve-year-old girl, with straight sun-bleached hair worn short, pale blue eyes, and a mild case of acne. She was the best junior tennis player in town.

"You won't believe this, it's so nutty. That camp they all went to, you know?"

"The one they're reuning about."

"Yes. Well, it hasn't been a camp for years. I guess it just sits there. So Miss Davenport had this brainstorm about reviving it, starting up a camp like the one they went to. She says if you look in the *New York Times* under ads for camps, all you see is Fat Camps, Tennis Camps, Swim Camps, Speech Defect Camps, Stuttering Camps . . ."

"Stuttering is a speech defect."

"And French camps. She says the world is ready for a good old-fashioned all-around camp for normal girls."

"Like the one they went to, no doubt. What was its name?"

"Allegro."

Kim threw herself full-length on the floor and stretched. "I've heard of people carrying on about their old colleges and even boarding schools, but *camps*?"

Stella looked down at her, grinning. "I know. I guess it was really sort of super, the way they talk about it. And they've stayed friends, so many of them."

"They aren't really going to start it up again, are they?"

"Oh, I don't know. It would cost a bundle. That's

part of the reason for the reunion; Miss Davenport wants to scrounge contributions out of the Old Girls."

Kim yawned. "Sentiment is one thing, money is another."

The phone rang, and Stella reached across the bed to get it. "Hello? Oh, hi, Nicky." She looked at Kim and made a face.

Kim indicated acute nausea. She got up and walked to the window, staring out at the early snow that had ruined her plans for tennis.

"Really, Nicky?" Stella managed to sound polite and immeasurably bored at the same time. "How exciting, I mean wow! Inscribed and everything. When are you going out there to visit him? . . . Yeah, I know. School spoils everything." She lay back on the pillows, balancing the phone on her chest while she examined her nails. In a minute she picked up the phone again. "What? . . . Oh, we must have been cut off. Listen, Nicky, my mother is yelling her lungs out. I've really got to go. . . . You bet, Nicky. So long." Stella hung up and shook her dark hair forward until it covered her face. She groaned. "That creep."

"What now?"

"She says she just got an autographed picture from the Fonze. And it says, 'To My Dear Cousin Nicole, All my love, Henry Winkler.'"

"Oh, sure. Oh, absolutely."

"She offered to show it to me."

"Stell, she can't be the cousin of every good-looking actor in Hollywood. I mean it stands to reason."

"Well, she has that letter from Erik Estrada, and the postcard from Donnie Osmond."

"I just don't believe it."

"Evidence is evidence. That's what my father says."

"Maybe in court, but not when it comes to Neecole Nasby. I don't know how she does it, but somehow it's a fraud."

Stella clapped her hands over her ears. "Oh, there they go."

Kim opened the door wider and stood listening as the voices of half a dozen women floated up the stairs in song. They were singing a sprightly little tune whose words were:

> "We're Allegro born, we're Allegro bred,
> And when we die, we're Allegro dead,
> So rah rah for Camp Allegro,
> Rah rah for Camp Allegro,
> Rah rah for Camp Allegro, rah rah rah."

Kim grinned. "I think that's kind of neat."

"Last year Mrs. Owens stayed with us for the reunion, and she blew reveille every morning. I nearly went through the roof."

"You mean on a bugle?"

"On a bugle."

Kim shook her head. "Most of the time your mother is such a sensible woman."

"'To each his own mania,' my father says."

The sound of voices talking and laughing grew louder as the women came into the hall. Some of them were leaving, and it seemed to Stella that they sounded even more revved up than usual.

"I'll talk to my Harriet about counseling," one of them called back. "She's on the swimming team at Radcliffe."

"Wonderful." It was Miss Davenport's voice, and it sounded excited.

"Joe will be in touch with you about the land deal," Mrs. Jesse's voice said above the hubbub. "He'll see we don't get taken."

And Stella's mother said, "We'd better get up there as soon as we can, Bertha, and see what can be salvaged in the way of equipment. The tent platforms, I should think, and of course Point House and the Inn and the Cottage are still standing."

"The wharf needs repair," Mrs. Jesse said. "We drove in last summer."

"Harry said he'd be glad to handle the legal end," Stella's mother said.

Somebody's voice rang out in the refrain again: ". . . and when I die, I'm Allegro dead . . ." Her voice faded, and the front door slammed. A car started up outside, and then another.

Stella stared at Kim in horror. "They're actually going to do it."

"I can't believe it. Won't their husbands stop them?"

"It sounds as if they're in on it. Kim! You know what that means?"

"What?"

"I'll have to go to Camp Allegro. Oh, my gosh." She

grabbed Kim by the sleeve of her T-shirt. "Listen, if I have to go, you have to go. I won't go without you."

"To a *girl's camp?* No way."

"If you're my friend, you'll go."

Kim scowled. "That's a rotten way to put it." She thought a minute and then brightened. "We'll just say no. We'll put our foot down."

"Do you think we could get away with it?"

"Of course. It's a free country, isn't it? I mean it's not a slave camp, after all."

Stella stiffened as she heard her mother's step on the stairs. Then there she was in the doorway, looking radiant. "Girls, you'll never guess what happened!"

"What, Mom?" Stella said, in a discouraged voice.

"We got it all together. We've raised the money for a down payment, and Davey is getting things rolling. We'll have an ad in the *New York Times* right after Christmas." She hugged them both. "You lucky kids. You'll get to go to Camp Allegro. And it's going to be, as much as possible, just the way it was. Davey will see to that."

"Oh, I don't think my mother would let me go, Mrs. Greene," Kim said.

"Yes, darling, she will. I talked to her last night. And I'll talk to some of the other mothers. That Mrs. Nasby, for one. We'll get a lot of your friends to go. I'm so happy for you."

When she had gone, the two girls stared at each other in despair.

"We're dead," Kim said.

2

On the first day of July, forty-eight girls and twelve counselors ran through the rain from the shelter of their tents toward the wide wooden steps that led down the hill to Point House. Some of them wore the ponchos that the catalogue had recommended, but more of them braved the wet in their navy blue shorts and the white T-shirt that said ALLEGRO in green letters across the front.

The curtain of rain nearly hid the lake that lapped around the foundation of Point House. The building, which had originally been a dance hall before the first Camp Allegro appropriated it, was a low, gray-shingled building built on a point of land. Its wide porch hung out over the lake, and on a clear day Loon Island was visible, about three-quarters of a mile ahead, and far beyond that, at the end of the lake, the hazy outline of the village. On the shore to the right of them was the tree under which the poet e.e. cummings had spent summers when Stella's mother was a camper. She claimed to have seen him once.

Stella and Kim sat down in the first row of folding wooden chairs, their backs to the big fieldstone fireplace, where a fire now burned to take the chill off the room. There were windows all the way around, and an old piano stood at the far end.

Kim gave Stella a poke in the ribs as Nicky Nasby pushed through a group of girls to sit beside Stella. She shook the rain off her regulation poncho and said, "Wow, it's really wet."

Kim leaned forward and looked at her solemnly. "No kidding, is it, Nicky?"

Nicky was a pretty girl, perhaps a touch too plump, with a tendency to let her face fall into a pout. She glanced quickly at Kim and said, "I wish you would please call me by my real name, Kim. 'Nicky' is a childhood nickname, which I would like to drop. My name is Nicole."

"Oh, sorry. Right. I'll try to remember, Neeeecole."

Nicky gave her a venomous look, and Kim sat back with a wicked grin.

There was a stir as three men came into the room and stood at the back, leaning against the wall and trying to look as if they didn't notice the commotion they were causing. One of them was about thirty, a handsome man with curly blond hair and a T-shirt that had the letters PRT across the front. His name was Goldsworthy; he was the tennis instructor. Kim's and Stella's tentmate, Judy, was disappointed to learn that PRT stood for Princeton Rifle Team, not Philadelphia Rapid Transit. Judy was from Philadelphia.

The other two men were younger, both of them undergraduates at Williams College. They were Ned and Harry, and they were "the help." Maintenance men, Miss Davenport called them. Stella had pointed out to Kim and Judy that Satan was known as "Old Ned" and also as "Old Harry."

"So?" Kim said.

"No comment."

Silence fell on the group as Miss Davenport strode in and faced them, smiling. She was a tall, athletic-looking woman, who was headmistress of a small girls' school in the winter. She looked them over with the practiced eye of her profession and gave a little nod that seemed to say she found them satisfactory.

"Girls, welcome to Camp Allegro." She waited for the tentative applause to die down. "This is a moving moment for me. I won't bore you with my own personal nostalgia, but as most of you know, I was first a camper and then junior counselor and finally volleyball counselor in this camp. We were very happy here, and I hope and expect you will be happy also. I would like to give you in a capsule the essence of the camp: self-control, self-discipline, enjoyment, consideration for others. We have no rigid regimen here, but there are certain rules I expect you to follow. You will obey the bugler's calls for reveille, soupie, assembly, rest hour, and taps. Are there any questions so far?" She nodded to a small, timid girl who raised her hand. "Yes?"

"What's soupie?"

"Meals." She turned to a girl who held a bugle in her lap. "Alice, play it for them."

Alice stood up and played the mess call. When she finished, Miss Davenport thanked her. "We used to sing along with it. 'Soupie, soupie, soupie, up at the Inn'—" She abandoned her song, and Stella grinned, remembering the rest of it: Where we soon assemble, make an awful din . . .

Miss Davenport introduced the twelve counselors, and explained the programs in arts and crafts, horseback riding, tennis, swimming. No one, repeat, no one must swim except during the hour allowed for it. "We don't want any accidents. Remember, girls, not even one toe in the water."

When she had finished explaining the necessity of quiet during rest hour and after taps, she asked for questions. Nicky raised her hand. "Yes, Nicole?"

Nicky pulled something out of her pocket and held it out. "I found it down there," she pointed toward the porch, "under the Point House on that little kind of pebbly beach."

"What is it?" Miss Davenport came over to her and held out her hand.

"A silver dollar."

Miss Davenport frowned. "Someone must have dropped it years ago."

"It's a Susan Anthony dollar. They've only made them lately."

Miss Davenport studied it. "Well," she said, "some picnicker I suppose. All right, girls, you're dismissed.

Remember, you are free till soupie. You'll want to unpack and get your tents in order." She waved an airy hand. "That's all."

Amid the confusion of scraping chairs and girls' voices, Nicole said distinctly, "My mother wouldn't want me to be someplace where there are bums hanging around."

Miss Davenport returned the Anthony dollar. "There are no bums, I can assure you, Nicole. Save your dollar for a memento of your first Allegro summer." She walked off and joined a cluster of counselors.

"I'll bet it's hoboes," Nicky said. "Or gypsies."

"Well, they aren't here now," Stella said sharply. She felt the need to defend Allegro.

"Silver dollars don't grow on trees. Or on scrub oak either." Nicky managed a flounce with her poncho and took off with her head in the air.

3

Stella eased her back against the rough bark of a white pine beside the tennis court and waited for Kim to finish her set with Mr. Goldsworthy. It was well past the hours for tennis instruction, but "Mr. Goldy," as he had quickly been nicknamed, liked to taper off by playing with Kim, who was by far the best player in camp. And Kim of course was delighted to play with him. It was pleasant to watch them, Stella thought, they were both so skillfull and graceful. The hypnotic effect of watching the ball as it slammed back and forth across the net, the soft plunking sound it made against their racquets, and the late afternoon heat made Stella drowsy.

They were into their third week of camp, and it still surprised her to find that she liked it so much. Her two big enthusiasms were horseback riding and writing for the weekly "Racket," the paper that was read to the campers each Sunday evening in Point House. She had become the star reporter, specializing in accounts of trips and activities that were meant to make the campers laugh. Last week she had written a kind of ghost story, about some spooky happenings that had taken place around camp in the last few weeks. One night her tentmate Judy had been sure she saw a ghost down on the dock. She couldn't tell anyone about it except her friends, because she was not supposed to be wandering around after taps.

"I couldn't sleep," she told Stella, "and I just thought I'd walk along the lake path. And I swear, there was this figure out on the dock. Whoever it was heard me coming, and they took off running."

"Ghosts don't run," Stella told her. "It was probably one of the men. They aren't supposed to be over here after taps."

Then Kim had found a place where the ground had been dug up recently, beyond the tennis courts. No one had figured out how the hole got there. Judy suggested it was an especially athletic gopher.

Stella brushed away a mosquito that sang loudly in her ear and rubbed her back against the tree trunk to ease an itch. She wondered if this could be one of the trees her mother had planted. She'd heard the story a million times about the summer they came back to camp to find that a forest fire had destroyed nearly all the pines, and only the bushy scrub oak thrived. All that summer the two nature teams, the Blues and the Greens, hacked away at the scrub oak and planted pine seedlings. "We beat the Greens," her mother said, "but between us we must have planted a thousand trees."

The scrub oak still persisted, but there were many

tall white pines on the camp property. They were pretty, but Stella liked the gaunt asymmetrical pitch pines best. There was one out past the Inn, on a slope overlooking the lake, where there was a built-in bench. Hardly anyone ever went there but Stella, who liked to use it as a hideaway. Last week, though, she had been puzzled to find a newly dug hole not far from her tree, like the one by the courts, and she could not imagine who had dug it or why. Several odd, spooky things had been happening lately. One night recently when the others were sound asleep, she was sure she had heard the kind of clink-plink sound that a shovel makes hitting rock. It sounded far away, so it could have been something altogether different, maybe a whippoorwill hammering away at a tree, or something. She hadn't mentioned it to anyone, but it had stayed in her mind.

She had written a poem about her pitch pine for the "Racket," and Nicole had said, "What a peculiar subject. Pitch pines are ugly."

In spite of Kim's and Stella's opinion of Nicole, the girl had made quite an impression on many of the campers. They liked to come and look at the autographed photographs of glamorous stars that she had tacked to her tentpole, and to listen to her airy accounts of this cousin and that cousin, this dear friend, that chum of her mother's. Stella had never met Nicole's mother, but she pictured her as a fading movie star. Kim said that was nonsense, but the woman must have been *something* in the movies or television, since they seemed to know everybody.

As she was thinking about Nicole, the girl appeared, walking toward the tennis courts, racquet in hand. She was not good at sports. She swam badly, dived not at all, always dropped the ball in volleyball, and could not learn to post on a horse. But she was worst of all at tennis. As Kim liked to say, "You could count on one finger the number of times Nicole returns the ball."

She was wearing clean, pressed tennis shorts, and she looked as if she had spent some time arranging her thick dark hair. Ignoring Stella, she walked to the edge of the court and stood there until Mr. Goldy, who was about to serve, looked at her and said, "Hi, Nicole. Were you looking for me?"

"I don't want to interrupt anything," Nicole said in her sweetest voice.

Stella muttered to herself, "The heck you don't." She had watched this maneuver before. Nicole had a crush on Mr. Goldy, and she hung around him as much as she could.

"I was just hoping," she was saying, "that you could give me a few pointers. I'm so slow to catch on, but I do want to learn to play a good game." She paused and added, "Like Kim."

Even from where she sat, Stella could see Mr. Goldy's sigh. And Kim was frozen in an attitude of silent rage.

Mr. Goldy walked to the net and said, "Maybe tomorrow, Kim."

Between gritted teeth Kim said, "Sure," and stalked off the court. She walked away, past the little store where the mail was delivered and soft drinks and boxes of raisins and sunflower seeds were sold for half an hour after rest hour. She strode down the sandy road that led past the baseball field and the riding ring to the county road. Stella had to run to catch up with her.

Kim was slicing the tops off the weeds as she walked, and she was quietly and fluently cursing Nicole Nasby, her mother, her movie stars, her ancestors, her posterity.

"Wait up," Stella said, but Kim didn't slow down. They walked along in silence, stirring up little clouds of sand. Johnny, the riding instructor, and two of her beginners were going around and around the riding ring, the campers riding bareback, as Johnny tried to teach them to grip with their knees. In the humming, hot silence of late afternoon, her voice reached them. "With your knees, Sally, with your knees. Rhoda, don't grab his mane."

Stella waved, but Kim did not even glance in their direction. The road past the baseball field was hilly, and Stella was breathing hard as she kept up with Kim's pace.

A cloud of dust rose ahead of them, and then a bicycle came up over the rise. It was Herbert, the boy from the village who rode over three times a week to clean out the stables. Herbert was about sixteen, and as Johnny said of him, "The spirit is willing but the IQ is weak." He did what he was told to do, but somehow he never finished his job, and Johnny herself usually had to do it. "He's my Hercules," Johnny said, "cleaning the Augean stables." Stella had been pleased that she understood the allusion, especially since no one else seemed to.

"Hiya," Herbert said, bringing his bike to a halt. He was a brawny boy, muscular, sunburned, and short. "Where ya goin'?"

Kim walked on, but Stella paused to be polite. "We're just getting a little exercise."

He chuckled. "Thought you girls'd get enough exercise without you have to go for a walk." He spun the pedal under his right foot. "Mind you don't go off the property." He was mimicking Miss Davenport, who constantly reminded the girls that it was absolutely forbidden to leave the camp property without a counselor.

"Oh, we won't," Stella said. She started to walk on. She would have to run again to catch up with Kim.

Herbert called after her. "Look out you don't run into the robber."

Stella waved. She had no idea what he was talking about; probably Herbert's version of the bogeyman. He really was a bit odd. She was out of breath again when she caught up with Kim, almost out to the county road. She slowed down, expecting Kim to wheel around and start back. Instead Kim marched across the road, looking neither one way nor the other, and disappeared from sight on the overgrown path that led to Moore's Pond.

"Kim!" Stella hesitated, called again, and getting no

answer, ran after her friend. It was one thing to be mad at Nicole for breaking up her game; it was something else to go breaking rules and getting into trouble.

The whole camp had gone to Moore's Pond for a cookout the week before, so Stella was familiar with the path. The pond was the result of a dam, still in place, where apparently someone had once had a mill, many years ago. It had been deserted even when her mother was a camper. It was rather a spooky place, with a wrecked and overturned rowboat lying in the grass, and a long-abandoned shack set a little way back from the dam. The vine-covered foundations of the mill were damp and slimy with age and algae. Miss Davenport said it had been traditional for the director to tell the girls a ghost story after it got dark. She had fulfilled the tradition, and the girls had shivered in spite of the mildness and great age of the story Miss Davenport told them. It was not so much the story that made them look quickly over their shoulders as the air of mystery and spookiness in the place itself. On the way home Johnny had spoken of the chthonian myth of the Greeks that described places haunted by spirits of the underworld. "Nowadays we say something has happened in a place like this, and the energies remain."

"Maybe somebody was murdered there," said Judy.

Johnny had laughed. "Maybe so. Or perhaps somebody just hated someone else so hard, we still feel the reverberations."

Stella thought about that now, and wondered if

Kim intended to add her hatred to the chthonian forces of the mill site. The notion scared her and she called out loudly, "Kim! Wait!"

She broke into a run, ignoring the low branches that lashed at her like malevolent whips. She came up over a rise so fast, she nearly fell into Kim, who had stopped.

She was alarmed and angry. "Kim, what do you think you're doing?"

"Walking off a temper tantrum," Kim said, with surprising mildness.

"We're off limits."

"Oh, so what. I just feel like walking. I'll be back before Alice blows warning for soupie." She started on again.

"You'll get in trouble. Miss Church will find out."

"Not unless you tell."

Stella hesitated. She did not like to break rules. Rules made her feel comfortable, secure. But Kim was her friend; she couldn't let her go off by herself. She sighed and followed.

In about fifteen minutes they came to the pond. Even in daylight it struck Stella as brooding and evil. The green water was so still, it looked almost solid. Dragonflies skimmed its surface, and Stella remembered the old wives' tale about darning needles that sew up your mouth. Instinctively she closed her mouth a little tighter.

Kim walked around the pond and sat down on the edge of the high concrete dam, dangling her feet.

Heights made Stella nervous. She watched Kim for a minute, and then sat down at the edge of the dam, where she could be on solid ground. "I don't blame you for being mad," she said. "Nicole is a pain."

"She's done that three times this week," Kim said. "She can't stand it for anybody else to have Mr. Goldy's attention. I mean he's the only one I can have a decent game with. I just want to play some decent tennis. I get all tied up in knots when I can't play tennis." She threw a fist-sized rock at the pond and it disappeared with only a small splash. "That water looks like thick pea soup. I hate pea soup. It makes me feel nauseated just to look at it."

"Then let's stop looking at it and go back. Kim, it's getting late." In the dense woods that surrounded them it already looked like night. "I hate it here."

"Do you? I think it's kind of cool. Like some place in a little kid's fairy story. You expect a frog to turn into a prince or something." Just as she said it, a frog leaped from a lily pad into the water with a green splash. Kim laughed. "See? Right on cue." She sighed and got to her feet. "I guess you're right. We better go back. I feel a little better. It must have been the prince that cheered me up." She walked across the narrow dam with the casual grace of a tightrope walker. As she came off the dam, she tossed a pebble at the rotting rowboat. "Wonder if that thing would float at all?"

"I shouldn't think so."

"Let's try it sometime."

Stella shuddered, picturing them slowly sinking in a rotten boat into pea soup water. "No thanks."

Kim touched the boat with her foot. "Just the same, I think I'll try it sometime. The bottom looks fairly sound."

A sudden loud noise seemed to make the dense, hot air vibrate, an unidentifiable noise halfway between a great cough and a growl. The girls froze where they stood and stared at each other.

"What was that?" Stella whispered. Her hands were wet.

It came again, from somewhere in the direction of the old shack. This time Stella grabbed Kim's arm and they ran.

When they were safely on camp grounds again, hot and breathless, they slowed down.

"What was it?" Stella said again.

"Gosh, I don't know. They don't have bears around here, do they?"

"I don't know. I didn't think so."

"Maybe it was the wind."

"There wasn't a breath of wind."

Kim was recovering her composure faster than Stella was. "Well, whatever. Some kind of animal, I suppose. And we can't ask, because we aren't supposed to be there."

Stella was ashamed of herself because she was still so frightened. To cover it up, she kicked at Herbert's bicycle tracks. "Maybe it was Herbert's bogeyman."

4

Stella sat in her usual hideaway on the little wooden bench that had been built long ago between two trees. The only visible evidence that Camp Allegro existed were the boat dock below her and the slanting green roof of the Inn behind her. She could just make out the top of the latticed tower attached to the rear of the Inn next to the counselor's room. In the tower was an enormous bell that the first director of the camp had hung there for the purpose of alerting the whole camp in a hurry if necessary. She had had it installed after the forest fire. That fire had occurred fortunately after camp, when no one was left except the director and her daughter and the maintenance men who were busy closing up. The fire had been checked before it reached the camp buildings, but it had been frighteningly close. As far as Stella knew, the bell had never been used; no emergency sufficiently drastic had occurred. But the key to the enclosure still hung by the door in the counselor's room, or so her counselor said. Campers were not allowed in the counselor's room.

That was their "sanity restoration room," Miss Church said. Miss Church, Stella's and Kim's counselor, was the nature counselor, and the only one in camp except the director old enough to be called "Miss." She was the biology teacher at Miss Davenport's school. The girls liked her, but she was eccentric. Bird walks sometimes absorbed her so completely that she forgot the girls she took along. Some of the more adventurous would sneak off while Miss Church was holding her breath over a sighting. If they rejoined the trip before it was over, they were safe, for Miss Church counted noses before and after, and forgot about them in between.

Sometimes Stella and Kim became exasperated with Miss Church, especially when she stood at the back of the tent just before taps calling loudly, "Girls! Stella! Kim! Judy! Have you brushed your teeth? Come quickly and brush your teeth before taps, girls." That clarion call was a source of amusement to the others, and someone had quickly dubbed them "The Girls in Tooth Tent."

But at the moment Stella was feeling tolerant toward Miss Church, mainly because she had not seen her for two days. Johnny had taken a group of five, including Stella, on an overnight horseback ride. They had just returned, happily too late to enjoy rest hour, so Stella was ensconced in her favorite spot, still wearing her jodphurs and boots, hot and sweaty and smelling horsey but very content. She was jotting down notes for an account of the trip for the "Racket." They had ridden all the way to Lake Chocorua and spent the night in sleeping bags on the shore. Johnny had let her cook the hamburgers over the open fire on the beach. In the morning they had had an early campfire breakfast and ridden to the top of the hill where they could look back on the jewel of a lake that narrowed in the middle, "like a pair of waterwings," Johnny said, and the towering mass of Mount Chocorua facing them as the sun rose. It was a sight Stella would never forget. All day she had been composing poems in her mind. If only she could get it right. Words were so inadequate sometimes, at least her words seemed to be. In the margin of her notes she wrote, "Mighty mountain, lift your arms and greet the sun . . . ." No, too trite. She crossed it out. When your soul was stirred, how did you say it?

She leaned her head back against the trunk of the birch and looked up through the lacy branches. The muscles in her thighs ached from the long ride, and she had a blister on the inside of one knee, but how happy she was. In fifteen minutes Alice would blow the end of rest hour, and it would be time to get out of her clothes and into a damp bathing suit, shivering with delight and discomfort at the same moment, and to race down the pine-needled path in her bare feet, wait on the dock, jiggling in impatience until Hen Norton blew the whistle that released them from landlocked creatures to inhabitants of the chilly lake. She shivered in anticipation at the deliciousness of it. Her swan dive was getting pretty good. Hen had complimented her on Monday. She longed to be able to dive like Hen, in fact to look like Hen or be like her, both of which were impossible goals. Hen, so nicknamed because of her initials, was tall and beautifully built with red-gold hair and eyes that matched her hair. She was funny, witty, and self-mocking, and she never lost her cool. At least as far as Stella knew. She played piano for vespers and special assemblies, and her music made Stella feel as if she were floating disembodied just above the surface of the silver lake.

She could see the Presidentials from here. Mt. Washington, Madison, and the rest, blue and insubstantial in the distance. She made a note: "Write poem about floating mountains."

She eased her feet out of her boots and stretched her toes. Very faintly she could hear music from the radio in the counselor's room. The Inn was far enough away from the girl's tents so that the counselors really did have some privacy. They took turns policing the tents during rest hour, one counselor to every two tents, alternating each day, so that every other day they had a free hour. Stella thought she would rather like to be a counselor when she was old enough.

She heard a few blows from a hammer, far off, which stopped abruptly, and she smiled. Harry was fixing the broken latticework that framed the structure of Point House beneath the porch. Someone must have shushed him, reminded him it was rest hour. He was always forgetting. Harry was nice. Nicole had a crush on him, too, and tagged around after him, embarrassing him sometimes. His attention was focused on Johnny, whom he admired so much that he even helped her swab out the stable when Herbert failed her. Greater love hath no man, Stella thought. Johnny took his adoration with her usual cool graciousness.

Stella looked at her watch, stretched, and leaned forward to put on her boots again. Time to go down and change. She could see Alice's small figure coming up the path to the Inn, where she blew her bugle. Then Alice was out of sight, and again for a last moment Stella drank in the solitude and peace. She stood up and something flew past her head and hit a tree. Startled, she bent to see what it was. It was a good-sized rock.

"What in the world?" She turned to look back, and another rock hit her a glancing blow on the forehead. Blood gushed out and dripped into her eye. Another rock and another came at her. She turned and ran, stumbling over underbrush, slipping on pine needles. She could hear the rocks striking the ground behind her.

5

"And you're sure you didn't see or hear anyone?" Miss Davenport hovered beside her with anxious face as the camp nurse removed the bandage she had put on the day before, examined the wound, and put on a fresh gauze pad.

For what seemed to Stella the fifteenth time, she said, "No, I didn't hear a thing or see anyone. The woods are pretty dense up there, you know."

"Well, we've had the area searched. The policeman from the village thought he found tramped-down brush, but the ground is too dry for tracks. I just can't imagine . . ."

"Probably some hoodlums from the village," the nurse said. "Don't worry so, Davey."

"Who wouldn't worry," Miss Davenport said sharply. "One of my girls attacked, and Mary Greene's daughter, at that. Mary will think I was careless."

"Oh, she won't, Miss Davenport," Stella said. "How could it possibly be your fault?"

"At any rate I shall tell the girls that that area is off limits from now on. It's too remote altogether."

Stella's heart sank. No more visits to her favorite

hideaway? "If I had shouted, they would have heard me in the counselor's room."

"There is no guarantee that anyone would be in the counselor's room. No, Stella, I must ask you not to go back there."

When she had gone, the nurse said, "Cheer up. There's another ninety-nine acres available to you. Are you going to be in the regatta tonight?"

"No, I'll be audience."

Kim was involved in the regatta, however. For days she had spent her spare time working on the decorations for her canoe. Boat Night was an old Allegro tradition. The canoes were elaborately decorated to look like anything from Chinese junks to Viking ships, and then after dark, illuminated by Japanese lanterns, they paddled past the beach. The best one got a prize.

Stella pulled her sweat shirt around her shoulders, tying the sleeves in front, and settled down near the end of the dock to watch the canoes. They were lining up down near Point House, ready to paddle in single file up the shoreline and past the dock, where the judges would choose the winner. Mr. Goldy, Hen, and the arts and crafts counselor sat on the diving board with clipboards and pencils. Behind them on the beach Harry and Ned were building a big bonfire, and Mrs. Erlandson, the cook, was bustling around preparing large kettles of cocoa and opening boxes of marshmallows that the campers would toast over the fire later.

Stella's gaze went for a moment to the rise in the land that hid her favorite bench. She had respected

Miss Davenport's request that she talk as little as possible about the stoning, to avoid panicking the girls, but she thought about it a great deal. When she had told Kim, and had said, "It was probably some kids," Kim's eyebrows had shot up. She said, "We're a fur piece from the village."

"Well, kids do run around in cars, or boats for that matter."

"You'd have seen any strange boats."

"Well, I don't know, Kim. All I know is, I got bombarded." Her tone had been sharp enough to stop the conversation. She had not meant to squelch Kim, but the whole thing bothered her, and she could not discuss it casually, as if it were something she had seen on TV. It was scary, and it had happened to her.

Judy came and sat down beside her. "Looks like they're about set." She had been down at the Point House shore. "Kim's in third place. Her canoe looks super. Your friend Nicole is second in line."

"Wouldn't you know she'd one-up Kim."

Someone called out, "Here they come," and there was a surge forward as they all strained to see.

It was a clear night, with a slight breeze and a quarter moon riding the sky like a slice of cloud. The stars looked scrubbed to brilliance. The canoes came slowly around the Point, each one lit with Japanese lanterns strung along a rigging from bow to stern. The first canoe was meant to be a Chinese junk, with papier-maché dragon's head for a prow. Nicole's was a Venetian boat, with a square-rigged pink sail made from some sheets hastily dispatched to her by her mother for the occasion. It had a pennant flying from the stern, a white flag with a red crusaders' cross. Nicole had done a good job, and her canoe brought applause from the crowd.

Kim's also brought a gasp of appreciation. She had fashioned a Mexican butterfly boat, and the result was simple but charming. It dipped slightly in the breeze like a real, hovering butterfly.

The long line of slowly moving canoes passed the dock, went as far as the next point of land, turned gracefully and started back. The judges were scribbling on their notepads. Everyone was quiet.

Once more they went as far as Point House, turned and came back. One of Kelly Hastings's Japanese lanterns came loose and fell into the water with a hiss. There was an "ohh" of sympathy from the crowd.

When the canoes had passed the dock again, Mr. Goldy picked up the megaphone and called out the names of the three top contenders. His voice boomed across the water. "Sheila Jackson, clipper ship." He paused. "Nicole Nasby, Venetian barque." Another pause. Stella held her breath. "Kim Wilson, butterfly boat." Stella breathed again. "Will you three please come past the dock again? The rest of you return to the Point House, circle around, come back and beach your canoes. You are all splendid. Thank you very much."

The three contenders broke out of the line and formed a line of their own. Nicole leading, then Kim, then Sheila. They paddled slowly by the dock, turned and came back. The judges huddled.

Mr. Goldy called out, "We're narrowed down to Nicole and Kim. Thank you very much, Sheila, beautiful job."

Sheila got a hand as she dropped out of the line and joined the others who were beaching their canoes.

Stella jumped down off the dock and waded into the shallow water so she could see better. If she had not been where she was at that moment, she would not have seen Nicole's paddle thrust out and under the keel of Kim's canoe as they made their turn to come back past the dock. It worked. The canoe flipped over on its side so quickly that it took a moment for the crowd to realize what had happened. Stella saw Kim's head come up above the surface and then she saw the wet sail wrap itself around her. Kim was struggling to free herself.

Stella ran forward into deeper water, but before she had gone more than a couple of splashing steps, Hen Norton took a running dive off the dock and in two or three strong strokes reached Kim and got her untangled.

When Kim was brought ashore, she was coughing and wheezing, partly, Stella knew, with rage. Somebody wrapped a blanket around her and led her to the fire. She sat there shivering, her eyelashes stuck together and her short hair plastered to her head. She pointed a shaking finger at Nicole, who had brought her canoe in and was saying, "Kim, what a shame."

"You did it on purpose," Kim said in a low, hoarse voice.

Nicole raised her own voice, glancing around to see if people had heard. "Kim, honey, what a rotten shame. I think I'd have won anyway, but you certainly should have had second. But I guess they do count seamanship too, don't they."

Kim hunched forward in a convulsive jerk, as if she meant to leap to her feet and strangle Nicole on the spot. Stella put her hand on Kim's cold arm. Other girls were standing around looking curious or uncomfortable or amused, depending on their natures. Mrs. Erlandson was speaking briskly about cocoa and cookies.

When everyone was sitting around the fire, Mr. Goldy rose and said, "The decision of the judges is . . ." He paused, and Nicole smiled. ". . . that first place should be divided between Nicole and Kim."

Nicole's face darkened, and she turned away, muttering something under her breath.

"You all did a great job," Mr. Goldy went on. "It was a beautiful sight, and we congratulate you all. Now let's dive in to that good-smelling cocoa and stuff that Mrs. Erlandson has there."

Hen Norton eased herself into position just behind Nicole and close to where Stella sat. Stella heard her say in a low voice, "Buck up, Nicole. Be a good sport. You were lucky to come off that well, all things considered." And Stella smiled to herself, for she knew that Hen too had seen what happened.

6

Charmaine Ellis and Ned were caught after taps out at the baseball field, kissing. Ned was fired, and Charmaine, who was one of the older girls, was closeted with Miss Davenport in the cottage for over an hour. She came out with a tear-stained face. She was not sent home, but for many days she was very subdued, and she never even bent one of the camp rules again.

"I think that's kind of impressive," Kim said to Stella. "I mean when Davenport gave us all that hoo-rah-rah about self-control and self-discipline and rules at the beginning of camp, I thought it would never work. But it has worked pretty darned well. Maybe it's the novelty, I don't know."

"Who told on Charmaine, do you know?"

"Nobody. Ginny Stegnar said Charmaine told her Davenport was out for a walk, late. It was just Charmaine's tough luck that Davenport had insomnia that night. They walked right into her."

They were stretched out on their cots, feeling lazy after a good swim. Miss Church was out somewhere, and Judy was in basketry class. The sound of hammering came up from Point House. Theirs was the tent at the top of the long flight of log steps that led down the hill, so they were more aware of what went on in and around Point House than the other campers were.

"That sounds like Harry banging away on the lattice again."

"It is, somebody broke it down, and he's madder than a wet hen."

"Who broke it? Why would anybody want to do that?"

"Judy thinks it's some animal, maybe a porcupine or something."

"They couldn't do that."

Kim rolled over and yawned. "Well, I don't know, or actually care."

Stella giggled. "Maybe it was Nicole looking for another silver dollar."

"Or maybe it was Nicole's gypsy."

Herbert walked down the path, past them and down the steps. He was working full time, since Ned's dismissal. Stella sat up and frowned. "Doesn't that dope know he's supposed to yell out 'Man coming'? We could have been lying around here with nothing on."

"Maybe that's what he had in mind."

"I don't think Herbert has much of anything in mind."

They got up and began to wash their hands in the big metal wash basin as Alice's bugle rang out warning. They took turns, splashing water from the big pitcher into the basin. Miss Davenport had bowed to progress sufficiently to install showers in the communal bath building, but she drew the line at running water or electricity in the tents. The girls washed in cold water that they carried to their tents, and they used flashlights for light. It was surprising how quickly they had grown used to it.

Mrs. Erlandson had cooked a particularly good dinner that night. Afterward some of the girls stayed in the dining room to help cut up watermelons for watermelon pickle. Mrs. Erlandson had been the cook when Stella's mother was at camp, and Stella had heard mouth-watering stories of the banquet on the last night of camp, when the season's awards were given out. Watermelon pickle was one of the accoutrements of the occasion.

Later Stella had lingered still longer, waiting for Kim to finish a set of tennis with Judy. She had joined Mrs. Erlandson on the back steps of the Inn, where Mrs. Erlandson had gone to cool off. They talked about the old days, and Mrs. Erlandson regaled her with stories of the escapades her mother's group had gotten into.

"I didn't know they were so wicked," Stella said. "I thought it was our generation that was so terrible."

"Not on your tintype," Mrs. Erlandson said emphatically. "You couldn't find a nicer bunch of girls than you kids. When people talk to me about kids today, I give 'em what-for." She mopped her damp face with her apron. "We got more crime than usual in the village and around hereabouts now, but that may be just 'cause we hear more about it, from them media folks."

"What kind of crime do you have?" Stella expected a tale of petty thieving or possibly wife-beating, but Mrs. Erlandson surprised her.

"We had a murder last Christmas."

"In the village?"

"Yep. Jake Fournier's wife up and stabbed him to death. Not that a person could hardly blame her. He was no good, Jake wasn't."

"Did they convict her?"

"Gave her ten years. Somethin' about self-defense or whatever you call it."

"Not premeditated murder," said Stella, whose father was an attorney.

"Probably she'd been meditatin' on it for years, but I dunno. Then we had that big bank robbery, but that was over to Center Ossipee."

"Did they catch him?"

"Nope, they didn't catch him. Some say the police around here couldn't catch a knock-kneed chicken, but that probably ain't fair. They searched all around the lake, but this is big, empty country. Anyways he got clear away, not a trace. Money never showed up either. My theory is, I think he hustled on up to Canada. That's what I'd do if I robbed a bank."

Stella laughed at the image of Mrs. Erlandson as a bank robber.

Mrs. Erlandson stood up and yawned. "Got to git on to bed. I'm makin' chocolate muffins for breakfast."

"My mother told me about your chocolate muffins."

"Probably rot your teeth, but the kids like 'em." She said good night and went inside to her room on the second floor of the Inn.

Stella wandered over to the tennis courts to wait for Kim. It was starting to get dark. I wonder, she thought, if Mrs. Fournier by any chance killed her husband over near Moore's Pond. That might have produced the chthonic vibrations Johnny was talking about. She would ask Mrs. Erlandson next time she talked to her.

7

In the middle of the night Stella was awakened by a noise. She sat up in bed and saw that Kim too was awake. Judy was sleeping soundly, and Miss Church was snoring. Kim got out of bed and came over to Stella's cot.

She whispered, "Did you hear it?"

"I heard something."

They sat still, listening. It was a cloudy night, with a smell of rain in the air. In fact Miss Church had talked about rolling down the tent sides before they went to bed, and then had decided against it, the girls promising they would wake up and do it if it really rained.

Between Miss Church's snores they heard the wind moving the boughs of the pines, and the faint splash of waves against the shore. Somewhere far off an outboard motor sputtered, died, and then came to life, making a barely audible rhythm in the muffled air. Out on the island a loon gave her eerie shriek, once and twice and still again. Then they heard the sound again. It was a thudding sound, like a rock against wood. Then a splintering noise. It came from the direction of Point House.

Kim grabbed her flannel bathrobe and thrust her arms into the sleeves.

"What are you doing?" Stella whispered.

"I'm going to see what it is."

"Don't be stupid. It's just some animal. Maybe a raccoon."

"So I'll find out. It bugs me. I can't get to sleep with all that going on. Besides, Harry will say the campers did it, if that lattice is broken again. And who're the ones that could get to it without being seen? Us."

Judy stirred, moaned, and turned over.

"Don't wake her," Kim whispered. "She always giggles."

Stella could think of few things she wanted to do less than climbing down the Point House steps in the pitch dark to find out what was making a mysterious noise, but she couldn't let Kim go alone. With a sigh she got out of her comfortable cot and put on her bathrobe. She fumbled on the floor by her cot for her flashlight. Kim was already out of the tent and heading for the steps. Next time, Stella thought, I'll pick a friend who's a scaredy-cat; then I won't get into these things.

Her slippers skidded on the pine needles, and she nearly fell. She clutched the wooden rail that bordered the steps and started down behind Kim.

When they reached the bottom of the stairs, they stood still, listening. Down here it was even darker than it had been up on the path. The windows of Point House looked like blind eyes, and the wide doors, usually left open, had been closed and bolted shut against the threat of rain. The building looked somehow menacing.

There was no sound other than the wind and the lake, and Stella was about to say, "Let's go back," when a sudden noise riveted them where they stood. It was unmistakably the sound of shattering wood.

Kim turned off her flashlight and started down the rocky slope between Point House and the lake. After a moment of hesitation Stella followed, but her heart was beating fast. She turned her flashlight around to make a weapon, and then wondered who she thought she was going to hit over the head. It must be a raccoon. She told herself this several times, as she slid and lurched down the slope. Her slippers were full of sand and pebbles. A nice raccoon, that was all. The pebble under her arch was cutting into her foot. She liked raccoons, although at home they made her father mad because they tipped over the garbage cans all the time.

She gasped with shock as Kim suddenly turned on her flashlight. She hadn't expected her to do that. The beam of light revealed that the dark green lattice, recently mended by Harry, had indeed been smashed open again. The rock that had done the work lay on the ground near the opening. Kim played her light back and forth, but there was nothing else to be seen. She bent down, preparing to go through the opening. Stella grabbed her arm.

"Don't go under there. It's probably full of awful spiders and things. Whatever animal broke the lattice is gone, or hiding in a corner somewhere . . . . Come on, let's go back to the tent."

Kim turned to answer her, and that moment a dark form lunged out of the opening, knocking Kim backward into Stella so hard that both of then fell in a heap. For just a moment they heard feet running, and then there was silence. Kim disentangled herself and sat up.

"My gosh!" Her eyes were wide. "What *was* that? It was big enough to be a bear."

Stella felt nauseated. She struggled to her feet. "Only bears don't wear glasses."

"What?"

"It was wearing glasses. I could see the reflection." Shock wore off, and panic took hold. "Come on!" She fled up the steps and fell into her bed, bathrobe, slippers and all, and pulled the blanket over her head.

"Girls?" Miss Church's voice said in her disoriented waking-up way. "Girls? Did you brush your teeth?"

"Yes, Miss Church," Kim said. "Everything's fine."

"Oh, good." Miss Church turned over, and soon the snores echoed through the night once more.

8

Stella woke up with a lurch of fear. Someone was bending over her. But it was only Miss Church. It was morning, and the rain was pouring. Miss Church was letting down the tent sides.

"Your blanket is all wet," she whispered. Then the first notes of reveille made whispering unnecessary, and she spoke aloud. "I knew I should have put down the sides last night."

"It's all right. I'll tie it down, Miss Church. Thank you."

Stella and Kim conferred in low voices as they sloshed through the rain to the Inn for breakfast.

They decided that Miss Davenport had to be told about the intruder, and that Stella would go to her alone. Kim was willing to go, but it seemed to Stella that it would be easier and that she would be less nervous if she went alone.

After breakfast and Mrs. Erlandson's splendid chocolate muffins, they hurried back to Point House for

Assembly. It was brief this morning, because Miss Davenport wanted them to get back to their tents and into dry clothes.

"So many of you simply ignore your ponchos," she said. "You really must not go around soaking wet. Riding and tennis will obviously be cancelled, but there will be the usual pottery and weaving classes here, and this evening we will have the musical program that Mrs. Endicott has prepared. Now please go straight to your tents and get into dry clothes, and WEAR YOUR PONCHOS."

After she had dutifully changed her shirt, Stella put on the cumbersome poncho and slogged through the water that ran down the path. With luck she would find Miss Davenport in the cottage.

As she knocked, Mrs. Erlandson came out, looking worried. Stella was surprised. She could not remember ever seeing Mrs. Erlandson anywhere but at the Inn. The nurse was there too, but she went into her office and closed the door.

Miss Davenport seemed preoccupied, but she said, "Sit down, Stella. What is it?" Miss Davenport had taken off her own poncho, but she still had on her yellow oilskin hat, which gave her an oddly rakish look.

Stella had trouble beginning, but Miss Davenport was starting to look impatient, so she took a deep breath and plunged in. By the time she was halfway through, Miss Davenport stopped her.

"Stella, do you mean to tell me that you and Kim were wandering around camp *after taps*?"

"We weren't wandering, Miss Davenport. We went to investigate this strange noise."

"I thought I made it clear at the beginning of the summer that no one, no one, for any reason, was to go anywhere at all except to the toilets. Didn't you understand that, Stella?"

Stella felt unjustly accused. "Yes, of course, but if something was *happening*. . . ."

"Then you should have roused Miss Church. It was not up to you to take charge. I am disappointed in you, Stella, you of all my girls I thought was responsible."

It was hard to contain her indignation. "Miss Davenport, it wasn't any *fun* going down there. I was scared spitless. We were just trying to find out what was wrong—"

Miss Davenport interrupted her. "And all you found was some animal that had broken the lattice again. Well, Harry will just have to build it better, that's all. He has too much to do, with Ned gone. And now someone will have to keep an eye on the supply room. . . ." She stopped, as if she had not meant to say that. She shook her head impatiently, and a drop of water rolled off the brim of her hat and down her long nose where it hung suspended for a second.

Stella tried not to look at Miss Davenport's nose. "What is wrong at the supply room?"

"Oh, nothing, I'm sure. Mrs. Erlandson has it in her head that some supplies have been taken, but that's absurd. Even the most mischievous camper is not going to carry off a twenty-pound sack of flour. She has just counted wrong, that's all. Please say nothing about it, Stella, nor about your escapades either. The girls love to dramatize things."

"Miss Davenport, it wasn't an animal."

"What was it then? A ghost? Really, Stella."

"It was a person."

"Person?" She looked blank.

"It wore glasses."

Miss Davenport sighed. "My dear Stella, on a night like last night, it would have been totally pitch dark down there. You could not have seen what bumped into you."

"I saw the glimmer of glasses."

Miss Davenport was growing exasperated. "What you saw, no doubt about it, was the eyes of an animal. They gleam in the dark. Now I am not going to punish you girls this time, but if I ever hear of your being out after taps again, Stella, I shall have to take serious steps. Now, I have a lot on my mind." She opened the door for Stella. At the last moment she said more pleasantly, "I do appreciate your honesty in coming to me. We all make mistakes, I'm sure."

As Stella went down the steps, the door was closing behind her. She heard the nurse saying, "I couldn't help overhearing, Davey. You don't think you ought to check up—?"

Miss Davenport's voice interrupted her, fierce and tense. "I cannot afford such a thought, Mildred. A rumor like that would wreck this camp." And the door closed, shutting off their voices.

9

"'We all make mistakes,'" Stella repeated bitterly. She and Kim were alone in their tent, with rain drumming on the canvas. "She just didn't believe me."

"I'm not surprised," Kim said.

"Why not?"

"She can't admit it. I mean she *can't*." She bent over and struggled with the wet shoelace on her sneakers. "I mean, consider it: if she accepts the fact that a strange man was prowling around camp after dark, what does she do? She has to call the cops. What happens? The kids all tell their mamas, and the mamas swoop down on the camp and snatch up their little darlings and take them home to safety. And there goes Camp Allegro, poof, up in smoke. Davenport can't take that. This camp is her lifelong dream."

"Well, I don't like not being believed."

Kim gave up on the knotted shoelace and pulled off the sneakers by force. She flopped on her back on the bed. "We've got to think."

"Should I write my mother about it?"

"No, she'd react just like Davenport. This camp is their lost girlhood. You can't mess with it."

"But the man could be an ax-murderer or something."

"Probably not. Nobody's dead. How do you know it was a man?"

Stella sat down. "I hadn't thought of that."

"It could even have been a camper, although I don't know what she'd be doing there." Kim sighed. "If only we could pin it on Nicole."

Judy came into the tent, dripping water, holding a newspaper over her head to protect her hair from the rain. She loomed in the opening of the tent for a moment, looking somehow bigger than she was. "Hey, you kids, what you doing?"

"What does it look like?" Kim said. "We're keeping dry. Keep your powder dry, boys. Don't shoot till you see the whites of their eyes."

"I was trying to practice my basketball shots, but Davenport drove me off. Why do you suppose Herbert is putting a lock on the supply room door? Does Dav expect us to steal the marshmallows?"

Kim looked interested. Stella had told her about the missing bag of flour. Bag of flour? It made no sense, now that she had time to think about it.

"He got it on upside down first." Judy chuckled. "That Herbert. I don't think he's retarded or anything, do you? I think he just doesn't pay attention. When you talk to him, he stops listening, about halfway through."

Stella picked up the damp newspaper. "I haven't seen a paper since we came to camp."

"It was in the counselor's room. I think Johnny brought it back when she went to talk to the blacksmith. It's several days old. Only a local paper anyway."

Kim said, "What were you doing in the counselor's room? We aren't allowed."

Judy shrugged. "Looking for something to hold over my head. There wasn't anybody there. When my hair gets wet, it gets so kinky, I can't comb it." She planted herself, feet apart, in front of the small mirror they all used and began to comb out her hair. She had tightly curly dark hair that hung to her shoulders.

"Cut it," Kim said. "No problem then. Hey, did you guys know that Eva Lynde cuts hair? She'll give you a trim for half a buck, or a real cut for a buck and a half."

"No kidding?" Judy said. "Is she good."

"Helen had hers done, and it looks okay. For two bucks she'll do something fancy."

"Like what?"

"Oh, I don't know, like make designs."

Judy burst out laughing. "I love it. Davenport would flip."

"For three dollars she'll shave your head. Completely."

"You're making it up," Stella said.

"No, honest. She's got a price list posted in her tent. Or she did have, till her counselor made her take it down."

"This camp is weird," Judy said. She bent her head

and studied it in the mirror. "I might get it cut short. My mother would kill me, but what could she do, after the fact."

Stella looked up from the paper. "They had a strawberry festival in Center Ossipee."

"Whee."

"Robert Redford is playing in Intervale."

"My father has a wolf album with Redford," Kim said.

"You mean he makes like a wolf?"

"No, he comments. The wolves howl."

Stella looked thoughtful. "I wonder if there are any wolves around here."

"I don't think so," Judy said. "Coyotes maybe."

"Coyotes with eyeglasses," Kim murmured.

Stella turned a page of the paper and gave a little gasp.

"What is it?" Kim said.

"Mrs. Erlandson's murderer is out on bail."

"Was Mrs. Erlandson murdered?" Judy said.

"This murderer she told me about. Mrs. Fournier, that murdered her husband."

Kim got up, acting casual, and drifted over to Stella's cot. She looked at the paper. "Where did she happen to murder him? Does it say?"

"No."

Judy turned to look at them. "You aren't scared about some woman that killed her old man, are you? It happens all the time. And they say people that kill their husbands or wives never kill anybody else."

Kim went back to her bed and stretched out on her back. "That's an interesting piece of information."

"Well, everybody knows. I mean it's a statistical fact."

"I meant about this Fournier woman being out loose."

"What's interesting about it?"

"Maybe I have a morbid interest in murderers."

"You're weird, Kim."

"You bet."

"Listen, I think I'll go see if Eva will cut my hair, before I lose my nerve. I mean it's raining, and I might as well. Anybody got a buck you can lend me till my allowance comes?"

Kim gave her a dollar, and when Judy had gone, she said, "I think I'll wander over to Moore's Pond and take another look around."

Stella gasped. "In the pouring rain?"

"Best time not to be noticed."

"But what for? What's there to see?"

"I don't know. There are just too many loose ends." She pulled on her poncho. "While you were talking to Davenport, I took a look down under Point House."

"And?"

"Well, the rain washed everything away of course, but inside, just inside the lattice, there's one faint footprint."

"Animal?"

"Not unless you know of an animal that wears gym shoes." She opened the tent flap. "See you later."

"You aren't going without me."

"I didn't think you'd want to go."

"I don't. I can't think of anything I'd hate to do more. But let's get going before Miss Church shows up."

"We'll go out by the tennis courts and the men's tent. That way we won't run into Davenport."

"We aren't supposed to go near the men's tent."

Crossly Kim said, "We aren't going near it. We're going by it. Are you coming or not?"

"It will be the end of me if we're caught. But all right."

Quickly they went out into the hard rain and took the long path that would lead them past the men's tent, the tennis court, and to the road. Stella hadn't had such knots in her stomach since the time she had had to play Grieg's Piano Sonata in the recital at home. The thought of home smote her. How far off it seemed and how safe. To cheer herself up, she began singing, "I'm Allegro born, I'm Allegro bred . . . ."

10

By the time they got to the area of the men's tent, the rain had lessened. Stella took a hasty look at the tent as they went by, but no one was in sight. It was crazy anyway, prohibiting girls to go near the tent in broad daylight; one of those rules left over from a quarter of a century ago. Though she had to admit to herself that she didn't like it when Herbert came barreling down the path past their tents. But that had to do with privacy. She said her thoughts aloud, and Kim said, "Who has privacy in a girl's camp?"

"Well, there's something about Herbert that makes me queasy."

Kim laughed. "Me too."

The tennis court was steaming as the pale sunlight trickled down through the last of the rain clouds. In the distance thunder echoed. "Crazy weather," Kim said.

"We've got to hurry to get over there and back by the time Alice blows soupie."

"We'll make it."

"I don't know why we're going."

"On a hunch. I've had this notion in the back of my head ever since we were there, that there's something important I only half noticed."

"What was it?"

"If I knew, I wouldn't be going back to look."

"Well, just so nobody sees us. I'm in enough hot water with Miss D. already. Both of us are, but I get a heavy dose because I'm her friend's daughter. Sometimes I get sick of this load of other people's nostalgia that we're carrying around."

Kim looked back. "I hope the courts are dry by tomorrow."

They hurried down the wet road, taking off their ponchos, which were suddenly stiflingly hot, and carrying them over their shoulders. The air was intensely humid and hard to breathe.

"We're going to get more rain, a thunderstorm, I think."

Kim nodded. "Guess so."

They went up the last incline before the county road, and Kim, who was slightly in the lead, came to a dead stop. "Oh, no!" she said. "Not her."

"Who?" Stella looked past her and saw Nicole standing in a grove of birches. She had not yet seen them. She seemed to be scanning the road that led from the village, as if she were looking for someone.

"We can't get by her without being seen," Stella said in a low voice.

"And she'll blab. Oh, that creep."

At that moment Nicole turned her head and saw them. For a moment she looked even more taken aback than they were. Then she recovered her poise and said, "What are you guys doing out here?"

"Exercising," Kim said shortly. "What are *you* doing here?"

She hesitated only a moment. "I was looking for that yellow-tufted chat Miss Church was talking about. It'd be points for my team."

"Yellow-breasted," Kim said.

"Whatever."

"In the pouring rain?" Stella asked.

Nicole looked up at the sky as if surprised. "Is it raining? It doesn't seem to be raining."

"But it must have been when you started out here."

Nicole flared up. "I suppose I have a right to be anywhere I want, *on the grounds,* without having to account to you two."

"I guess you have," Kim said. "We all have." She looked at the road. There was no way they could go to Moore's Pond now. If they ventured off the property, Nicole would run like a greyhound to tell Miss Davenport.

"We'd better be getting back," Stella said to Kim. "Almost time for warning." She emphasized the word "warning" slightly and saw that Kim understood her.

"See you," she said to Nicole. They started slowly back.

A shout stopped them. Herbert was riding his bike

up the road, standing up to pump harder. Nicole turned away, as if to go back, but Herbert was beside her in a moment, skidding his bike to a stop.

"Hi, Nicole. Sorry I'm late. My old man made me chop some wood. You been waitin' long? Hi, Stell; hi, Kim."

Nicole gave him a freezing glance. "I don't know what you're talking about." She walked quickly, past Herbert, past Stella and Kim.

Herbert looked crestfallen. "Gee, I didn't know she'd be mad. I've been late before, and she ain't got mad. I couldn't help it, could I, if my old man made me chop wood?"

Kim looked at him with obvious delight. "No, Herbert, of course you couldn't. Why don't you catch up with Nicky, make it up with her. You two are such good friends, I'm sure she'll forgive you. You two meet a lot out here, don't you."

"Well, pretty often lately." He stopped uncertainly, as if it had occurred to him that he might be revealing secrets. "Well, not *so* often."

"Just as long as you don't do it too often after taps. I mean you shouldn't get Nicole into trouble with Davenport."

"No, we give up on that, after she nearly caught us that time. Well, see ya." He pedaled off after Nicole.

Stella and Kim looked at each other.

"Ha!" Kim exploded. "Isn't *that* an interesting development!"

"But we aren't going to tell on her."

"No, but just let her try any tricky business with us after this."

"She'd just deny it."

"It would be easy to scare Herbert into a complete confession. Dates after dark, secret meetings.... where!"

As they talked, they heard Alice's bugle, which meant only fifteen minutes till dinner. Rather relieved, Stella said, "We can't go to the pond now."

"Tomorrow then. It'll keep."

That night after dinner Judy told Kim and Stella that Nicole had been spreading the story that Stella had kissed half the boys in the eighth grade and some high school kids too.

Stella stared at her in stunned amazement, and then she began to laugh.

Kim was red-faced with anger. "How can you laugh? That dirty rotten little liar . . . . Judy, did anyone believe her?"

"There are always a few people who believe that kind of stuff, but most of us know Stella too well to go for a dumb story like that. I mean there are at least ten kids here from you guys' home town."

Stella said, "I guess I shouldn't laugh. It just strikes me funny."

"It doesn't strike me funny," Kim said. "I'm going to have it out with her."

"No," Stella said, serious now. "You are not. You

are not going to talk about it. The only thing you can do with a silly story is ignore it."

"You could sue her for libel," Judy said.

"Don't be ridiculous. Just forget it." She sat down beside Kim, who was scowling fiercely at the floor. "It's really kind of pathetic. I mean if that's the only way a person can get attention . . . ."

"Yeah," Kim said sarcastically, "my heart breaks for her, she's so pathetic. She's a skunk, that's what she is."

"Maybe she has problems," Judy said. "What's her family like?"

Stella shrugged. "All she has is a mother. I've never met her."

"There you are. She's suffering from a one-parent family."

"Bull," Kim said. "She's suffering from an advanced case of the nasties, that's what she's suffering from." She flopped over on her face and wrapped her arms around her head. "Some day," she said in a muffled voice, "I'll get even."

"Does she really know all those stars?" Judy said. "I mean that really gives her prestige around here."

Kim turned over and sat up. "That gives me an idea."

"What?" Kim's ideas sometimes made Stella nervous.

"I just got this nifty idea." She put on her Adidas and jumped up from the cot. "Be back shortly."

She came back a few minutes before the assembly

call for the evening concert in Point House. She was grinning broadly.

"What have you been up to?" Stella said. "You better comb your hair. It's time for the concert. Say, speaking of hair, weren't you going to get yours cut, Judy?"

"Eva was busy with some pottery project. 'Tomorrow,' she said. But where were you, Kim?"

"Listen," Kim said, "I remembered about Jackie Jones."

"What about her?"

"She studied handwriting. She has a book on it. I sneaked her over to Nicky's tent and showed her those photos that are all over the place." She paused dramatically.

"And?"

"The signatures on them are for real, but the other stuff, like 'To my dear cousin Nicole' and all that garbage, all that was written by one person."

Judy blinked. "But the writing looks different."

"She faked it. But Jackie showed me, it's all one person. The way she loops her long letters like *g*'s and *p*'s, the way she crosses her *t*'s . . . Don't you get it? Nicky sent for the photos, just like any fan. I've got one myself of Rod Stewart. And the pictures come autographed, and then she added that other stuff."

Judy and Stella looked at her for a moment. Then Stella said, "Oh, gosh, I think that's pathetic."

"So do I," Judy said. "She must be awful insecure."

"Insecure, my eye! She's just a big show-off." Kim

was disappointed at their reaction. "You two are soft in the head." She gave her hair an angry swipe with the comb and flounced out of the tent.

"She really doesn't like Nicole, does she," Judy said.

"They've always fought."

"Well, we'd better go."

Together they went down the steps to Point House.

It was a good concert, even Judy agreed. The music counselor was a gifted violinist, who played with a civic symphony orchestra in the winter. She played several pieces, including Debussy's "Golliwog Cakewalk," which the girls always enjoyed, and then Hen Norton played the Tschaikovsky B Minor Concerto. Johnny, the riding counselor, and Greg, who taught pottery, sang several duets. At the end Hen played some Gershwin, and then some Simon and Garfunkle songs that the campers could sing.

When the concert was over, the girls made a circle, as they always did at the end of an evening occasion in Point House. They linked arms and swayed to Hen's accompaniment, singing "Now the day is over, Night is drawing nigh, Shadows of the evening Steal across the sky. . . ."

As they finished "steal across the sky," a strident clanging shattered the quiet night. Everyone froze, startled and mystified. Then Miss Davenport broke away from the group with a look of terror. "The bell!" she said. "The alarm bell!"

The voices of some of the counselors cut across the

sudden panic. Stella heard Hen Norton and Johnny, who were near her, calling out, "To the Inn. Everybody to the Inn. Quietly. Double-file."

The bell continued its wild clamor as they started up the steps. The girls were puzzled and a little frightened, but they were in orderly pairs, not speaking much.

By the time they reached the Cottage, about halfway to the Inn, the clanging stopped. Miss Davenport hesitated, then halted them.

"Stay here please, while I see what it is. There is no sign of forest fire. Just stay here quietly till I come back." She strode off up the path, looking determined.

The girls waited what seemed an eternity. They talked some, in low tones, but no one panicked. Discipline, Stella thought, everybody keeping cool. It's what Miss Davenport was always harping on, and it was really working. Stella felt rather proud of her fellow-campers. She wished her mother could see how well they were behaving.

After some time Miss Davenport came back, Mrs. Erlandson with her, and Herbert bringing up the rear. She spoke to the girls. "Nothing seems to be wrong. The door to the bell enclosure had been unlocked and was standing open. Mrs. Erlandson was asleep upstairs. Herbert was at the stable. Harry and Mr. Goldy are in the village at a movie. No one saw anyone. I can only assume that some youngsters from the village wanted to play a trick on us."

Youngsters from the village, Stella thought. What a

good way to put it, making it sound like a harmless prank. But whoever rang that bell knew that the key hung in the counselors' room.

"Now go back to your tents and prepare for bed. There's nothing to worry about, no harm done at all. We'll take turns keeping watch at the Inn just so you won't feel nervous." She made her voice brighter than usual. "Good night. Go to sleep and dream of the lovely concert you just heard." She gave an airy wave. "God bless."

"That was a good performance," Kim said as they walked back to the tent. "She deserves an Oscar. Youngsters from the village, my eye."

"What do you think it was?"

"I don't know, but I intend to find out."

Stella lay awake long after taps, and after Miss Davenport had made her nightly tour with her flashlight, pausing to say good night at each tent and to make sure she heard four voices answering her. Thunder growled at the other end of the lake, and lightning played across the near mountains. Soon the rain began again, drumming a soft tattoo on the canvas sides of the tent. Somewhere in Camp Allegro there was someone who did not belong there.

11

Stella was making a list in her mind. She would have liked to discuss it with Kim, but Kim was asleep. Item: Someone had broken into the area under Point House at least twice. Item: Nicole had found a silver dollar there. Item: Someone or something had growled at them at Moore's Point. Item: Someone had thrown rocks at her. Item: Someone had stolen a bag of flour. Item: Someone had rung the bell when everyone was at Point House.

Maybe it was what Miss Davenport said, kids trying to harass the outsiders. Except perhaps for the rocks, nothing that had happened seemed dangerous or threatening. They were not the sort of acts you would expect from a woman who had murdered her husband, for instance, even if she were a little batty. Maybe it wasn't even one person who had done these things.

She was getting sleepy and she was beginning to accept Miss Davenport's theory. Kim had a hyperactive imagination, and she had let herself be influenced by it, but really, where was the evidence?

She sat bolt upright at a sudden sound, then lay back again, smiling at herself. A chipmunk had scampered down the roof of the tent over her head. She yawned. She was not going to see everything as menacing. It was ridiculous. The person under Point House could have been some vagrant who had found shelter there when the camp was deserted, and had come back not realizing the place was full of girls. If so, he must have been more frightened than they were. As for the noise at Moore's Pond, no doubt it *was* an animal. There must be a few bears left in New Hampshire. Kids from the village, probably, threw the rocks to scare her, just for the fun of it. And maybe the same vagrant or another one stole the flour.

She came wide awake again. She had forgotten to account for the bell. How could she have let that slip out of her mind, when it had just happened? Perhaps because it was the hardest to explain. Kids from the village or vagrants would not know that the key to the bell enclosure hung from a nail in the counselors' room. Perhaps it was a practical joke, unrelated to the other things. Part of the trouble with logic, her father said, was trying to see a pattern where there wasn't any. What if one of the men had rung the bell, just for the heck of it? Not Mr. Goldy, of course, he was too responsible, and anyway he had been at the movies with Harry. Herbert? He could have done it. Or he could have told some of his village chums about the bell and the key. Maybe some of the village people really wanted to get rid of the camp, scare them off. She had heard that often the natives of a place resented intruders. Maybe the deserted camp had been a good place to kiss your girl, or hide from your parents, or whatever the village kids liked to do.

The chipmunk raced down the tent roof again. "Good night, chipmunk," she murmured. "Keep watch." The rain had stopped. She considered rolling up her tent side to get more air, but decided she was too sleepy.

And then it was reveille, and the sun was out, and clouds of steam rose from the wet tent. She got up quickly, to get a chance to comb her hair before Judy planted her bulk in front of the mirror. Judy was infinitely good-natured but she was unpushable. Stella remembered that Judy was going to get her hair cut today and she rejoiced. She hoped that Eva would cut it practically off, so it wouldn't take Judy so long to comb it every morning.

Kim waylaid her after flag raising. "I've got a plan for getting to Moore's Pond. Legitimate."

"How?"

"We'll ask Miss Church to take us there on a bird walk."

Stella groaned.

"Well, it would give us a chance to look around."

"What are we looking for?"

"It's right on the edge of my mind that there's something funny about that old boat."

"Of course there is. It's shot to pieces. It's rotting."

"I mean something different about it from the other time we were there."

Stella shook her head. "Kim, we aren't the only people who go to Moore's Pond. Probably any number of kids go there on picnics or to fish or whatever."

"So?"

"So they moved the boat."

"I don't think moving it is what bothers me."

"What is it then?"

"If I knew, I wouldn't have to go look."

Stella sighed. "Going on a bird walk will mean getting up before dawn."

"It won't kill you. But if you don't want to go, you don't have to."

"You mean just you and Church would go? A bird walk of two?"

"Oh, she'll probably ask for volunteers. That doesn't matter. It might be better, in fact. I could do my investigating without attracting her attention."

"Nothing attracts her attention when she's birding. Except birds."

"Then you'll go," Kim said, illogically. "Here she comes. Miss Church? Miss Church, Stella and I are dying to go on a bird walk to Moore's Pond."

Miss Church's face lit up. "Moore's Pond?"

"Yes. The last time we were there, I mean the night we had the cookout, you know, I thought I saw what I think was a . . ." She hesitated for only a moment. ". . . a scissor-tailed flycatcher."

"Truly? Oh, splendid. Did he go wheeeep? and then . . ." She lowered her voice to a dramatic throaty tone. ". . . prrrreet?"

"That was it," Kim said. "I'm sure of it."

Stella crossed her fingers and hid her hand in the pocket of her shorts. Kim should go on the stage.

"I haven't seen one around here this year. That would be worth the trip, wouldn't it."

"Do let's go, please," Kim said. "How about tomorrow?"

Miss Church considered it. "Very well. Will you girls get up when I call you? I'll set my watch alarm, so we won't disturb anyone." They were at the Inn steps, and she turned to a group behind them. "Judy dear, will you join us?"

"For what, Miss Church?"

"Kim and Stella and I are going on a bird walk to Moore's Pond tomorrow morning."

Judy shuddered. "No, thanks, Miss Church. I'm no good at early rising."

Nicole pushed forward, her face sharp with interest. "You guys on a bird walk? You're kidding."

"Nicole, they are quite serious. Kim thinks she saw a scissor-tailed flycatcher at Moore's Pond."

"When?" Nicole said, squinting at Kim.

"The night of the cookout, of course," Kim said.

"Oh? Are they out at night? If birds are wandering around at night, how come we go bird watching before dawn?"

"Because that's when it is easiest to apprehend

them." Miss Church was enthusiastic about the prospective trip. "I'll announce it at assembly, in case others would like to go."

"I'll go," Nicole said.

Kim said, "Before dawn, Nicole. You know you hate to get up early."

"I don't either. I often get up before dawn."

"Then we have at least four of us," Miss Church said happily.

"Nicole will chicken out," Kim said.

Nicole flushed with anger. "I will not. Do you think you're the only one that's interested in that stupid nuthatch?"

"Not nuthatch, dear," Miss Church said. "Flycatcher."

"Scissor-tailed flycatcher," Kim said, enunciating each syllable as if she were speaking to a small child.

Between her teeth Nicole said, "I am mad about scissor-tailed flycatchers. It is my fav-or-ite bird." She turned her back on them and went up the steps to the inn.

"We're trapped," Stella said later to Kim.

"We aren't. Drum up trade. Get a bunch of kids to go. Bribe 'em, offer 'em a hot fudge sundae in the village, anything. If there's a crowd, I can operate without Nicole right on my back."

"That's what you think," Stella said.

12

Five girls walked silently behind Miss Church in the predawn grayness, Stella, Kim, Nicole, Eva Lynde, and Helen Blakewell. Eva was a small, dark-haired girl who, in Stella's sometimes discouraged opinion, always did everything right. It was inevitable that she would respond enthusiastically to Miss Church's call for bird walkers. Helen was thin and bespectacled, with stringy hair, and tried too hard at everything.

It was a cold morning, with autumn chill already in the air. Stella was glad she had worn her cords and at the last moment had slipped on her sweat shirt over her cotton shirt. Nicole was wearing shorts, and her legs were goose pimpled with cold.

Every now and then Miss Church turned back and put her finger to her lips, although except for an occasional snapped twig and the soft pad of footsteps on pine needles, the girls were making no noise.

Birds were making sleepy sounds in the trees, and Miss Church's binoculars were lifted eagerly again and again, though she could not have seen much yet.

As they passed the Inn and headed out the road that led away from camp, the golden rim of the sun came up over the eastern mountains. Miss Church hustled them along, anxious to get to Moore's Pond before it was fully light.

Stella and Kim had laid a plan. Whichever one of them found it easiest to move away from the others would examine the boat. "Lift it up if you can," Kim said, "and look under it. I've got this hunch. And look everywhere else, too. I want another look in that cabin."

If they had no opportunity to do as much searching as they wanted to, it was agreed that Stella would "remember" something she had left behind, a notebook perhaps, and would run back to get it while the others started on home.

"Why me?" Stella said at first. "You're the one that's so keyed up about that darned boat."

"Because I've got a hunch Nicole will be right on my back every minute. She's only going because she thinks we're up to something. She's hardly the bird walk type."

And she had been right. Nicole stuck close to Kim all the way, eyeing her sharply and suspiciously from time to time, for, as Stella was thinking, Nicole knew perfectly well that Kim was not the bird walk type either.

The densely wooded road to the Pond was still dark and not a little creepy. Stella shuddered when a branch caught her in the face or a wet leaf plastered itself against her neck. She imagined enormous spiders everywhere. There were no rattlesnakes around here as far as she knew, but there were others: garter snakes, bull snakes, blacksnakes, hog-nosed snakes, whatever. She knew they were harmless, but that didn't mean she looked forward to stepping on one. She glanced nervously at the branches she was walking under. Her mother liked to tell about the time she held a garter snake, and earned points for her nature team. Well, maybe Stella could hold a garter snake for ten seconds, to get points, but no more. And she would wash her hands thoroughly afterward. Her dad said the fear of snakes was psychological. Maybe so.

She was glad when they came out of the woods into the clear area by the pond. Miss Church was asking Kim where she had seen the flycatcher, and Kim was making a convincing show of trying to remember precisely the tree. The two of them moved off, and in a minute Nicole followed them.

Eva yawned widely, and got out her notebook. Helen stubbed her toe over a root. She had already stubbed her toe eleven times, by Stella's count, sometimes on the camp road where there was nothing but sand to stumble over. Helen was not a model of coordination. Stella felt a little sorry for her, but not too much. A person shouldn't be so eager to please.

She wandered over to the old boat, pretending to be peering across the pond for possible birds. Helen followed her. She tried to look at the boat without seeming to. In a moment she saw what it was that had been bothering Kim. A piece of the gunwale had been recently replaced with an uneven scrap of wood crudely nailed on. Why would anyone bother to do that? There were cracks along the keel that would cause the boat to leak like a sieve and probably sink in a few minutes, so why bother to mend the gunwale? She thought about it, while pointing out to Helen a bird that just lifted out of a tree on the far side of the pond. She thought it was just a grackle or something, but she tried to look impressed to divert Helen.

The mended part of the boat rested on the ground. What if it had been mended so that the boat would rest evenly all the way around, making a sort of shelter, the kind of "house" kids liked to play with? That was probably it; some kids had slapped a piece of wood over the broken part and used the boat to play house or to hide things under. Nothing to Kim's hunch after all.

Thinking about the strange noise they had heard, she moved casually away from Helen, who had her field glasses fixed on the place where the bird had been, and wandered past the high dam structure to the shack. She pushed open the door with her foot. It pushed hard and made a track in the dusty floor. This time she did more than look in; she went in. It was not a pleasant place to be. Animals had used it, and the heap of refuse, gathered probably by a pack rat, smelled. As far as she could see, there was no indication that any human had been in there even to look around, for a long time. She pushed at a heap of dank leaves and saw something that glittered dully. She stooped for a closer look. It was a cheap can opener, dirty and rusted. Maybe someone had left it on some long-ago picnic, or perhaps the pack rat had found it and brought it here. It was of no interest to her either way.

She went out, glad to leave that close, dank air. To avoid Helen, who was glancing around in perplexity as if the birds had not cooperated, she went the other way, a little further toward the woods that bordered the pond and the remains of the mill. She looked down at the broken timbers and the excavated cellar. Part of a waterwheel lay on the ground. What had they done here anyway? What did people do in mills like this? Ground corn, maybe. It seemed an odd place for it, but what did she know about mills. Probably the water power they could harness here was the reason for it. A stream had obviously once flowed in here and over the dam, though now it was dry. In the cellar or whatever it was, a battered rough timber door closed off what looked like a space dug out of the hillside. If the building had been a house, she would have thought of the door as leading to a root cellar, like the one they had in *Little House on the Prairie*. But she shuddered to think what it must be like on the other side of that door now. Mold, mildew, spiders, rats, rotting wood, damp earth. Perhaps after all, she thought, I am not an adventurous outdoor type like Mother. Maybe I am more like a city girl. For a moment she thought with longing of a cool, clean little city restaurant that served hot fudge sundaes with toasted almonds.

The sun was up now and it was growing warmer. She put up her arms to take off her sweat shirt. As she got it halfway off, her head and face covered, she was suddenly grabbed from behind. She tried to cry out, but the sweat shirt muffled her, and a moment later a large hand was clapped over her mouth, almost choking her with the cloth of her shirt. Her arms were twisted painfully behind her back and quickly tied. She was dragged off into the woods.

13

She tried to scream, but the hand held her sweat shirt clamped over her face. It was difficult to breathe. Some kind of thin rope or perhaps vine bound her wrists tightly enough to make them ache. She struggled, but she was held in a strong grip. Branches snapped against her as she was dragged further into the woods. She prayed that Miss Church or Kim or one of the others would wander over to these woods in their pursuit of birds, but it seemed like a dim hope. This particular clump of trees was tangled and almost impenetrable with vines and low-growing bushes, not a place one would go from choice.

The length of time before they came to a stop seemed like hours, though it could only have been a few minutes. She was dumped on the ground like a sack of meal and then propped against a tree. Her hands were untied, then retied in front of her. During the few seconds that they were untied, she tried to fight loose, but the person holding her gave an angry grunt and held her back with his knee while he tied her up again. Another rope went around her waist, tying her to the tree trunk, and one around her head to hold the shirt in place. Then nothing happened.

She sat very still, trying to tell whether her captor had left her or was still there. She couldn't hear breathing or any human sound, but she had the sense of being watched. She was almost too frightened to think. In the course of being dragged to this place, she had been quite certain that this was the mysterious person they had been stalking, some kind of demented hobo, who lived like a hermit in the woods and resented being spied on. If she could only talk to him, perhaps she could get him to let her go. She had great faith in the power of reasoning. But there was no way she could speak. He had secured her sweat shirt over her face so that she could make no sound except a low growl in her throat. The thing that bound her head seemed like cloth, like a scarf or a necktie, rather than rope or vines. It stifled without cutting into her. The shirt was loose enough over her nose so that she could breathe a little, but the effect was so claustrophobic that she had to fight down panic. She almost wished she would faint. Instead she made herself sit quietly, breathing as shallowly as possible, willing Kim to come looking for her. Miss Church wouldn't miss her until they started back, unless someone said she was missing. Even so, she could imagine Miss Church saying, "She's only looking for birds, dear. Don't disturb her."

She tried to think of the possible plans her captor

might have for her. Perhaps he meant to scare the campers away from here. Perhaps he meant to do her physical harm after the others had gone. Perhaps he meant to kill her. She started to count in French. It was an old childhood device for keeping down fear. Un, deux, trois, quatre, cinq, six, sept, huit, neuf. . . .

She stiffened. She had heard a twig break. She listened intently. She didn't hear anything more, but suddenly something hard was held against the side of her neck. It felt like a gun, but she wasn't sure. A hoarse voice spoke, a voice that sounded rusty like an old spring.

"Don' you come here no more, none of you. You come 'round here again, me, I kill you dead. You hear me?"

Stella swallowed and tried to speak. "I hear you." The words were muffled by her sweat shirt.

She was untied and jerked to her feet, the gun still hard on her neck. Her hands were untied. She was seized roughly by the arm and propelled forward through the brush.

In a few minutes she heard a faint voice calling her. It sounded like Kim. Then Miss Church's voice rose above it. "Stella! Stella, we're going back now, dear. Stella, don't hold us up."

The man twisted her arm until she moaned. "You go now. You look back, I shoot you." He gave her a hard push, and she stumbled forward.

Trying to fight her way out of her sweat shirt so she could see, she kept moving as fast as she could, stumbling over everything in her way. Just as she got the shirt off over her head, she saw Miss Church and Kim.

"Oh, there you are. Really, Stella, you shouldn't go off so far that you can't hear me call. If we don't hurry we'll be late for breakfast. Nicole? Eva? Helen? Are we ready now?" The other three joined them.

Kim was staring at Stella. In a low voice she said, "What happened? You look as if you'd seen a ghost."

Stella found her voice. "I did. Tell you later."

Nicole was watching them suspiciously. Helen and Eva trailed along behind Miss Church, Helen eagerly recounting her sighting of some bird or other.

"I know you kids are up to something," Nicole said. "Don't think I won't find out what it is." She turned and threw a significant look at the old boat.

Stella didn't try to talk on the way back to camp. She was trembling so, it was hard to keep up. Kim walked beside her, watching her with an anxious eye.

"What are those marks on your wrists?" Kim said.

Stella looked down at her wrists. It had been vines; she could see the green that had come off.

"You're breathing funny," Kim said.

Stella shook her head. She was glad she was breathing at all.

It was not until after assembly that Kim and Stella found a chance to talk alone. "What happened, for Pete's sake?" Kim said. "You look terrible."

Stella told her. Kim's mouth fell open.

"Stell!"

"Yes."

"I never expected anything like that. Listen, I could have got you killed or hurt or something. I'm sorry."

"Never mind that," Stella said. "The thing is, what are we going to do?"

Kim thought. "We have to tell somebody. I mean that wasn't just ringing a bell or throwing a few stones or stealing a bag of flour. By the way, I found the flour."

"Found it! Where?"

"Under the boat."

"Under the boat?"

"Yeah. There might have been other stuff too, I don't know. I had to leave it because Nicole came along. She had her eagle eye on me all morning. She knew I'd been looking under the boat, so she tried it, but she lifted the bow end, and she couldn't get it up very far because the whole thing is so waterlogged, it weighs a ton. The flour is under the stern end. Anyway I don't think she saw it. She's just trying to figure out why I'm interested in that boat."

Stella was quiet for a few minutes, trying to put things together. She rubbed her chafed wrists. "So there's this man who steals flour, hangs out over there in the woods, and doesn't want us around."

"The question is, who is he?"

"Maybe just a tramp, a hermit. This camp was deserted for so long, it was probably pretty handy. He could sleep in Point House or the Inn or the Cottage in bad weather. Pretty cushy. Then we come along, and he's forced out."

"It seems like a little more than that. I mean just a harmless hermit isn't going to threaten to kill you, and he wouldn't have a gun."

"Well, he might. He must have to depend on game for food, if he's really a true hermit."

"Who should we tell?"

"Well, not Miss Davenport. I don't want to go through that again."

"Mr. Goldy?"

Stella considered it. "I don't think so. He'd probably get a gun and go after whoever it is. He might get himself shot. I don't think that hermit is playing games."

"Johnny?"

"Possibly." Stella thought a moment. "How about Hen Norton? She's only a couple of years older than we are, so she's not going to come on strong like some adult. And you can trust her."

They agreed on Hen, but they could not tell her right away. She had just left with a group of campers on an overnight canoe trip.

"I guess one more day or so won't hurt," Kim said.

Stella rubbed the back of her neck. "I guess not."

14

All day Stella had to fight the impulse to look over her shoulder. She avoided being by herself, and she cancelled a riding hour because she didn't want to leave the grounds even with Johnny and the other riders. Kim stayed close to her most of the day.

The sun shone and the lake sparkled, and Stella wished she could get her fears out of her mind and enjoy herself, but she kept feeling that arm grabbing her and that rough hand over her face. She dreaded the coming of night.

Judy provided a diversion by appearing in the tent with her new haircut. Her long, hard-to-manage mass of hair was cut short to make a neat cap of tight curls. It was becoming, although it made her look quite different.

"Wait till you see this," she said. She showed them the back of her head, where Eva had left a tiny patch of scalp, roughly heart-shaped. "She says it's her trademark."

"Your mother will flip," Stella said. "A heart on your head!"

"It'll grow out before she sees me. I don't know if she'll like my hair short, but she'll get used to it. Present 'em with a fact is what I always say. Eva's doing a terrific business. Nicole's getting hers cut now."

"Nicole?" Kim said, raising an eyebrow. "You mean all them gor-jus locks are falling? Somebody ought to sweep them up and sell them for souvenirs. Get your Nicky-lock here, folks. Step right up for your luscious sausage-shaped me-men-to of the fabulous Nicole. Have it encased in bronze, hang it from your rearview mirror. No home should be without one."

Judy picked up the singsong refrain. "Somewhere in the world there may be a home without a Nicky-lock . . ."

"Knock it off." Stella spoke so sharply, both the girls looked at her in surprise. Then they turned to see what she was looking at behind them. Nicole stood there, her hair cut short, her face a mixture of fury and hurt.

"You miserable brats," she said. Her voice was higher than usual. "I'll get even with you if it takes my whole life." She swung around and half ran down the path toward her tent.

Defensively Kim said, "I didn't know she was there."

"Me either. I didn't mean for her to hear. I mean we were just kidding."

"Nicole isn't much for taking a joke," Stella said. It had been unpleasant; she wished it hadn't happened. She couldn't stand Nicole, but a person shouldn't be made fun of. Her father had given her a talk once about not destroying anyone's dignity, and it came back to her mind now. He had been talking about prisons at the time, but it applied.

When evening came, her fears caught her in a grip that she was ashamed of but couldn't shake off. It took a long time to fall asleep after Miss Davenport had said good night and her electric lantern had bobbed on up the path. The night seemed especially dark. She longed to run after Miss Davenport and ask permission to sleep at the Cottage. A girl was allowed to if she were ill or anything was wrong. But she was not sick, nothing was wrong that she could explain, and even if she did sleep there for one night, there would be the next night and the next. She pulled the blanket up under her chin and tried to think of pleasant things. But every snapped twig, every flap of a tent canvas, even the soft lapping of the lake on the shore, a sound she usually loved, made her tense. There was a light wind murmuring through the pine branches, and there was a chill in it. At home it was still hot, so her mother had written, but here in the last weeks of August the touch of winter could be felt. She shivered. Herbert had come to work wearing an old down-filled jacket, and at assembly Miss Davenport had sung them a little song that the campers used to sing in the old days:

> Brr, it's a cold day,
> Brr, it's a chilly day,
> When the mercury goes down.

It had a catchy tune, and although she couldn't remember any more of the words, those lines kept going through her head.

She gasped at an eerie sound and clutched the flashlight that was on the floor beside her, before she realized that it was just the loon again, a sound she ought to be familiar with by now. It came again and again, a blood-chilling scream like a woman in torment. Even though she knew what it was, she could not relax. She got up quietly and poured herself some cold water from the pitcher, drank some of it, and threw the rest out the side of her tent. Something scampered away. Chipmunk? Squirrel?

Again she fought for sleep, but it didn't come. Her eyes flew open as she sensed someone standing beside her. It was Kim.

"Push over," Kim whispered. "I can't sleep either. And I'm freezing."

With Kim crowded in beside her in the narrow cot, she was afraid she might fall out of bed, but at least she was not so frightened any more. Misery loves company, she thought. Kim went to sleep in a few minutes, and finally Stella did too.

In the morning Miss Church frowned at them. "You're not supposed to sleep together, girls. Those cots are too small."

"I was freezing, Miss Church," Kim said.

"Then stop at the Cottage after assembly and ask for another blanket. Get some for Judy and Stella, too."

All day Stella found herself looking up whenever anyone came along the path, hoping it was Hen back from the canoe trip. She needed to talk to her. For one thing she was afraid that if she were not stopped, Kim would take it into her head again to go back to Moore's Pond. Kim was not easily frightened, and her curiosity more than outweighed her caution. But by late afternoon Hen and her girls had not yet returned.

"They went down to the Saco," Kim said. "Anything might have delayed them. That's a fast river."

Harry had driven the truck to the place where the canoes would come at the end of their trip. Several times Stella wandered out to the road, looking for the truck, but there was no sign, no cloud of dust to tell her a car was coming.

Just before dinner she went out to the tennis court to watch the last of a game between Mr. Goldy and Kim and also to look one more time for the truck. Nicole and Helen were in the second court, batting balls back and forth without much enthusiasm. Nicole kept laughing a loud, artificial laugh and glancing toward Mr. Goldy to see if he noticed her vivacity. Mr. Goldy did not look at her after the first quick, startled glance. He played tennis seriously, just as Kim did, and he was not to be distracted.

Stella sat down on a bench to watch. For a moment she forgot her anxiety in the pleasure of watching them play. They were so good! She wondered if Kim would ever end up at Wimbledon or Forest Hills. Then she could say, "That's my best friend." Good old Kim.

Nicole missed Helen's serve for the fourth or fifth straight time and collapsed on the court laughing hysterically. Mr. Goldy looked annoyed at the hullabaloo. They were not playing a game, just volleying the ball, both of them missing it more often than not. Helen stumbled over the tape and almost fell flat. Mr. Goldy returned a shot, finishing a game, and moved up to the net to say something to Kim.

She gave Nicole and Helen a dark look and nodded. Then she and Mr. Goldy started to walk off the court. He stopped to lower the net, and Kim came over to Stella.

"Those stupid oafs," she said. "How can anyone play when they're over there shrieking like hyenas? If they don't want to play, why do they come out here?"

"To play up to Mr. Goldy," Stella said. She turned her head sharply at a sound. "It's the truck!" She jumped up and went out toward the road to look. Kim followed more slowly.

All they could see at first was a cloud of dust rising over the lift in the road.

Kim cocked her head. "It doesn't sound like the truck."

A car going too fast for the narrow road emerged. It was a blue Lincoln Continental; its shiny polish dimmed by a thin coat of sandy dust. That stuff leaves scratches, Stella thought; what a shame, on that beautiful car. Wondering idly whose mother it might be, or what friend of Miss Davenport's, she turned away. Kim kept watching.

The car slowed to a stop, and a tall, broad-shouldered woman in an expensive-looking white pantsuit with a scarlet blouse stepped out.

"Whose is *that*?" Kim said under her breath.

The woman was built on Amazonian lines, and her clothes fit her to perfection, but she had an extraordinary ugly face, heavy, broad-jawed, almost brutal-looking.

"Nobody I'd want to run into in the dark," Stella said. "She'd eat you up."

"And spit you out again," Kim added.

The woman looked around and then beckoned to them imperiously. "Where is everybody?" She had a deep voice, a smoker's voice that seemed about to cough at any moment.

It was a peculiar question. Stella said, "Well, all over. Who did you want to see?"

"My daughter, to begin with. And the Davenport woman." She was looking around, taking everything in. "My God, it doesn't look like all that money, does it?"

It seemed like a rhetorical question, so Stella didn't answer it. "Which one is your daughter?"

She shaded her eyes with a large hand and looked toward the tennis court. "I think that is mine, the one that's missing every ball that comes at her." She raised her voice to a bellow. "Nicole!"

Nicole, who had had her back to the road, dropped her racquet and whirled around. She stood absolutely still, as if stunned.

"Well," her mother yelled at her, "what are you standing there for, like a ninny? Come here and say hello to your mother. I've come eighty miles out of my way to see you."

Leaving her racquet where it had fallen, Nicole came toward her mother in a strange little half-trot, as if some hand were pulling her back at every step. Her face was drained white, and she looked somehow smaller, shrunken.

"Hello, Mother." Even her voice was different, small and thin like a child's voice. "What a nice surprise."

"Well, give us a kiss." The woman bent down and presented a cheek for a quick peck. "Good God, Nicole, what have you done to your hair? And you've gained ten pounds at least. I thought this place would get you in shape."

Stella and Kim moved away, unnoticed by Nicole or her mother. Helen, who had hung around expectantly waiting to be introduced, joined them.

"She's awfully big, isn't she," she said. "Nicole's mother."

"Monstrous," Kim said. She looked thoughtful.

Stella looked at Kim. "I feel terrible," she said.

"I know."

"Miss Davenport has aspirin," Helen said helpfully. "Have you got cramps or what, Stella?"

"Oh, Helen," Stella said, "do shut up."

15

Nicole's mother stayed for dinner. She sat at Miss Davenport's table, and her hoarse voice could be heard all over the dining room. Nicole, sitting beside her, seemed to shrink further and further into herself. She answered her mother's many peremptory questions in the same high, childish voice with which she had greeted her.

Miss Davenport did her best to be a good hostess, but she was distracted. The truck had not come back with the canoeists, and she was obviously worried. She kept glancing toward the door, and at every unexpected sound she looked up quickly.

At about nine o'clock Nicole's mother left, with a roar of the Lincoln's engine and a cloud of sand and pebbles. Nicole disappeared into her tent. And still the canoeists had not come back.

From their tent Stella and Kim could see the light in the Cottage where Miss Davenport waited long after taps. No one said much about the failure of the canoeing group to return, but there was a tension in the camp. Even Miss Church seemed abstracted. The Saco was a deep river with rapids in many places. Only girls who had passed their senior lifesaving tests were allowed to go on the trip. Even so, as they were all aware, accidents could happen.

It was nearly midnight when the sound of the truck reached them. Nearly everyone was still awake or else woke up quickly. "They're back!" "Hey, they're back." "Thank God, here they are." The phrases ran through the camp like a force suddenly let loose. For once counselors did not say, "Shh!" People got out of bed and stood in their pajamas, waiting to find out what had happened.

It seemed a long time before the girls came down the path, but apparently they had stopped at the Cottage to report to Miss Davenport. Two of the older girls, Ali Brewer and Esther Flannery, came first, looking bedraggled and tired, carrying soggy bedrolls. Ali's T-shirt was torn.

"What happened?" Kim said.

They answered without stopping. "Couple of canoes ditched in the rapids," Ali said. "Everybody's okay."

"We'll tell you tomorrow," Esther said. "We're beat."

"Back to bed, girls," Miss Church said. "Everyone is all right, praise be. Back to sleep now."

The others came down the path in ragged single file, silent except for an answering "hi" here and there. And finally, just as Stella was getting too sleepy to keep her eyes open any longer, Hen came, walking quickly and not looking left or right. Stella noticed that she limped. She hoped everything would be all right by tomorrow so she could talk to her about the Moore's Pond business.

At assembly in the morning Miss Davenport explained briefly what had happened. "I know you were all worried, but thank God all is well. Hazel's canoe struck a rock in the rapids and went over, and another canoe hit hers. All of the girls in both canoes were thrown into the river, but they are fine now." She smiled at Hazel, who had a bandage above her eye. "A little worse for wear perhaps, definitely damper, but safe." She went on to the day's announcements.

Hen was not there, and Stella was worried. Could Miss Davenport have blamed her? Sometimes some of the counselors skipped assembly, but Hen was usually there to make announcements about swimming scores, races, lifesaving classes.

After assembly she sought out Ali to ask her about the trip. All the girls who had been on it were being questioned by the other campers. Anything, Stella thought, to add a bit of drama to our lives.

"Hen was marvelous," Ali said. "She was out of her canoe and into those rapids in ten seconds flat. If she hadn't been so quick, there might have been a tragedy. Hazel was knocked out when her head hit the rock. Both canoes were wrecked."

"Miss Davenport doesn't want us to talk too much

about it," Esther said. "She's afraid the kids will build it up, and parents will be upset."

"Build it up." Ali made a face. "The real thing was built up enough for me."

It was not until the middle of the afternoon after swimming that Stella found Hen alone. She was lying on her cot, still in her bathing suit. She looked tired.

"Hi, Stell," she said. "Come on in. I suppose you want the story straight from the horse's mouth too."

"No, I've heard it ten times. I wanted to talk about something else." She hesitated. "But maybe later. You look tired."

"A little. Mostly depressed. I don't like to lose two canoes and come that close to somebody getting hurt."

"But it wasn't your fault. Everybody says you were terrific."

Hen smiled. "What did you want to talk about?"

Stella sat down on the end of the cot and told her about the things that had happened. When she came to the part about being tied up and blindfolded, Hen sat bolt upright.

"Holy cow! You should have told Davenport right away. Stella, that's serious."

"Well, she didn't believe me the last time. She doesn't want to think—"

Hen interrupted her. "She's gone to the village to see about getting a couple of secondhand canoes, but the minute she gets back, you must tell her. I'll go with you, to make sure she understands you're on the level. Stella, you could have been hurt." She pulled on a T-shirt and stood in front of the mirror combing her hair and frowning in perplexity. "Who could it be? Why does anybody want to scare us away from here? I mean that's taking a lot of chances. If all he wants is Point House to sleep in, you'd think it would occur to him that what he's doing might get him a bed in the county jail. Let's go talk to Kim. I want to hear more about that old boat. It doesn't make sense, does it?"

When they got to Stella's tent, Judy was there looking anxious.

With a sudden premonition of trouble, Stella said, "Where's Kim?"

"I'm supposed to tell you." She hesitated, looking at Hen. "Just you."

"It's all right. What *is* it, Judy?" She put her hand on Judy's arm and shook her a little.

"Well, I'm trying to tell you. Somebody came by and told Kim that Nicole and Herbert went over to Moore's Pond. It was supposed to be a big secret, only Kim was to be told—"

"Who told Kim?"

"Janice, Nicole's tentmate. Anyway Kim blew her top and tore out of here. She said something about Nicole might get her head blown off. What is it all about, Stell?"

Stella looked at Hen. "Kim's gone after them."

Hen didn't hesitate. "Let's go. We can take my

Honda." She was off toward the parking lot, her long legs covering the ground in a fast walk that was almost a run. Stella had to hurry to keep up.

"I'm coming too," Judy said. "Whatever is going on, I'm coming."

Stella didn't stop to argue. She climbed into the front seat of the Honda, and Judy pushed past her into the back. Hen drove up the road at a bone-jolting rate of speed. No one spoke.

As the little car came up over the last rise in the camp road, Stella gripped the door to keep from bouncing. Without slackening speed Hen crossed the county road and plunged into the narrow, stump-strewn track to the Pond. Branches snapped at the windows and scraped the top of the car as they banged along over the ruts. No car had been down this road for a long time.

They had to stop before they got to the Pond itself, because the road ended suddenly in a heap of sand and rubble. Hen jumped out, leaving the door open, and Stella and Judy were right behind her. Before they came out of the tangle of brush into view of the Pond or the dam, they were stopped in their tracks by the roar of a gun.

Hen motioned to the two girls to stay back, but they followed, bending low, as she did, to keep out of sight. The gun thundered again, and Stella muttered, "Darn you, don't you hurt Kim. Don't you dare hurt Kim."

Hen held out her hands to stop them. They could

see the Pond now. The boat was turned over. Kim sat on the ground with blood coming from her leg. Nicole stood in front of her facing the dam.

Indistinct in the late afternoon light, a man stood on the dam, holding a shotgun. It was impossible to tell what he looked like or whether he was young or old.

Hen yelled, making her voice so deep, Stella would not have recognized it. "We're coming in. You're surrounded. Throw down your gun and come out with your hands up."

The man stiffened and stood still for a moment. Then he jumped off the dam and ran into the woods where he had once dragged Stella.

Hen raced for the boat. She lifted Kim to her feet and said to Nicole, "Run for it. My car."

"No, I'll help you." Nicole put her arm around Kim on one side, Hen on the other, and Kim hopped along on one foot. Her left leg was dripping blood, and she looked deathly pale.

When they got to the car, Hen lifted Kim into the front seat, while the other three crowded into the back. "I'll look at it in a minute," Hen said to Kim. "We've got to get out of here."

"Yo," Kim said faintly, and closed her eyes.

Hen ran the Honda backward down the path, leaning out the window to watch for the track, getting hit repeatedly in the face with branches. It was a harrowing ride, and several times Stella was sure they were going to end up in a clump of bushes or even tip over.

The little car strained and protested but it kept going. Stella glanced at Nicole. Her face was white and set.

As soon as they reached the county road, Hen pulled the car to one side and bent down to examine Kim's leg. "Shotgun pellets." In answer to Kim's grunt she said, "I know how it hurts! I got a blast once myself. And you're bleeding like a stuck pig. But honey, you're all right." She pulled off her T-shirt and wrapped it tightly around the calf of Kim's leg. "Not the most modern method, but the T-shirt is clean. Can you kind of hold it in place, real tight? Good girl." She sat up, squared her tanned shoulders, and drove the car fast down the camp road.

16

The living room of the Cottage seemed very crowded. Miss Davenport still had not come back, but the camp nurse was carefully extracting shotgun pellets from Kim's leg. Johnny was on the phone trying to reach the Ossipee police. Hen was warming some milk on an electric plate. Nicole sat huddled in Miss Davenport's wing chair. Stella sat beside Kim, holding tight to her hand. Kim's face was gray and covered with a film of sweat, her teeth clenched against the pain.

"Are you sure she shouldn't have a shot of brandy?" Hen said, coming with the warm milk. "No, not indicated," the nurse said, her own teeth set as she tried to get the pellets out with the least damage to Kim. "Keep trying for Dr. Harris. If you can't locate him, tell the North Conway hospital I'll bring her into Emergency first thing in the morning. It looks okay to me, but I want an M.D. to check it. Only one more, Kim. You're being real brave."

Kim tried to smile, winced, and tightened her grip on Stella's hand till Stella had to bite her lip.

"Keep trying please, Operator," Johnny said. "It's very urgent." She hung up and tried the doctor's number. After a brief conversation she hung up. "Gone fishing." She called the hospital and made an early appointment.

Hen turned to Nicole. "Would you like some hot milk too, Nicole?"

Nicole shook her head.

"Try to tell us now just what happened, will you? It's still pretty confused."

Nicole took a deep trembling breath. "I asked Herbert to walk over to Moore's Pond with me. I know it's off limits, but there was something Kim was after and I wanted to beat her to it."

"Where is Herbert, by the way?" It was Judy, who had just come back into the room with gauze pads and a roll of adhesive that the nurse had sent her for.

Nicole looked at her. "He ran away."

"So what happened?" Hen persisted.

"Well, I'd seen Kim looking for something under that old boat, and I wanted to find it first. I didn't know what it was. I don't know if she knew either."

"Flour," Stella said.

"Yes, I saw the flour first, but then I turned the boat over, Herbert helped me, and there was this gunny sack. It was full of . . ." She paused, looking at them as if she could hardly believe her own words. ". . . full of money. Hundred dollar bills."

"Money!" Stella stared at her. "You're not making it up?"

"Would I make it up? Would I lie to you now, when I almost got Kim killed?"

"All right," Hen said soothingly. "Then what?"

"This man yelled at us. He had a funny voice, hoarse. Herbert grabbed a handful of money and ran."

Hen made a wry face. " 'Said adieu forevermore, my love, and adieu for evermore.' "

"The man was up on the dam, standing there aiming that gun at me. He yelled a few things, but I couldn't understand him. It seemed like a long time. I guess he couldn't decide what to do with me."

"Good heavens," Johnny said quietly.

"Then Kim came, all out of breath. She must have run all the way. See, I told Janice to tell Kim I'd gone. I wanted to show off. I wanted Kim to know I dared to go over there just as much as she did. When I saw her coming, I thought first she had come to drive me off. But I didn't care why she had come, I was so glad to see her. Then the man shot the gun over my head. I thought Kim would take off, the way Herbert did, but she came right over to where I was and grabbed my hand. She said, 'I think he'll have to reload or something, I'm not sure. Anyway let's duck down and run zigzag for the woods. Don't stop for anything.' And I was going to do what she said, because all of a sudden I saw what a hero Kim was and what a crumb I'd been and now I'd got her life in danger." Slow tears began to stream down her face. "So we crouched down and took about two steps, and he shot again and hit Kim in the leg." She mopped her face with the back of her hand.

Stella was looking at her. "You could still have tried to run."

"I couldn't leave Kim there like that."

Stella looked up at Hen. "She was standing in front of Kim when we got there, remember? Protecting her?"

The telephone rang, and Johnny grabbed it. "Yes? . . . Oh yes, I've been trying to get you. Listen, chief, we've had a shooting over here. This is Miriam Johnson, I'm a counselor at Camp Allegro, you know where it is? . . . All right. Miss Davenport, our director, is not here at the moment . . . ." She went on to give him a concise account of what had happened. Then she listened for a moment. "Hold on. I'll ask." To Stella and Nicole she said, "Can either of you describe him?"

Stella shook her head. "I never had a good look at him. But he talks funny, like maybe a Frenchman."

Nicole said, "About five feet eight, lots of beard and long hair, skinny. Glasses."

Johnny repeated the description into the phone. "Do you really think so? . . . Yes, fine, and can you send us a couple of men to keep an eye on the camp? . . . All right, thank you." She hung up. "He thinks it's some bank robber that ripped off a bank over there almost a year ago."

Stella looked at Kim. "Mrs. Erlandson's bank robber."

Hen looked out the window. "Kids are hanging

around. They know something's going on. Judy, go get Church. And no word to anyone; don't act mysterious either."

When Judy came back with Miss Church, Hen said, "We've had a slight accident, Miss Church, no problem. Will you get the girls to the dining room on schedule. Tell them Miss Davenport has been delayed and ask them to congregate at Point House after supper, and we'll have a sing-along."

"Don't give them any indication that anything's wrong," Johnny said.

Miss Church blinked several times. "What *is* wrong?" She stared at the nurse's hands as they deftly bandaged Kim's leg.

"Long story, Churchy," Hen said. "Fill you in later."

"Very well," Miss Church said. For a second Stella thought she was going to salute. "I'll carry on."

"Nicole, you and Judy and Stella had better go along to the Inn and get something to eat. Try to avoid looking as if the world has just ended." Hen smiled and patted Nicole's wet cheek.

Nicole took a deep breath that ended as a sob. "I don't want to eat anything. I can't face them. If only I hadn't—"

Hen stopped her. "Honey, the road to futility is paved with 'if only I hadn'ts.' We all have them. Everything is turning out okay, so don't turn yourself into a tragic figure." She leaned over quickly and gave Nicole a hug. "No, that wasn't fair. I just mean, don't take it so big. Kim is going to be fine, the cops will catch the robber, the bank will get its money back, and you kids will be heroines."

Johnny said, "Wait till Davey hears about the publicity. There are bound to be reporters."

"Oh, publicity my foot," Hen said. "She wants an image of the camp kids as self-reliant and disciplined and brave and resourceful, and by gosh, they were. Everybody risking everybody's neck for everybody else and catching a robber to boot."

"He's not caught yet," the nurse said.

"Oh, they'll get him. They're calling out the highway patrol and half the lawmen in the state. It'd be a good time to rob a bank, if any of you are so inclined."

Alice's bugle call for supper rang out from the Inn.

"There goes soupie," Johnny said. She looked at Stella and Judy.

Stella shook her head. "I want to stay with Kim."

"I'll stay too," Nicole said.

"Well," Judy said, "I don't like to seem unfeeling, but I am going to fall flat on my face if I don't eat pretty soon."

Johnny laughed. "Good girl. Remember, fend off the questions, but don't act as if you're concealing anything. We'll talk to them later at Point House."

"I am the kid who doesn't know nothin'." She gave Kim a sympathetic pat and left.

Hen said, "We *do* have kids who are self-reliant, disciplined, brave, et cetera, et cetera. I'm proud of them." She helped the nurse pick up loose ends of bandage that had been cut off. "I don't see how it will hurt the camp any. No parents in their right heads are going to think that a lurking bank robber is a chronic situation."

"Point House," Kim said in a faint voice.

They looked at her questioningly.

"I think she means there might be more money stashed under Point House," Stella said. "We found him there, you know."

"And we all assumed he was a tramp looking for a place to lay his weary head." Hen looked at Johnny. "We'd better tell the boys in blue to keep an eye on Point House."

"Let's tell Goldy and Harry," Johnny said. "They'll never forgive us if they don't get in on the act. Kim, sweetie, you try to get some sleep. We'll be right here. I don't think we could budge Stella loose. I'll go up and scrounge some food from Erlandson for these kids, and then I'll help Church round up the gang after supper. We've got to tell them some of this before the gendarmes descend."

"I'll keep a lookout for Davey up at the parking lot," Hen said. "She's got to be informed pronto. Where do you suppose she is?"

"She said she might go on up to Intervale, about the canoes, if she couldn't get a good deal in Madison."

In a few minutes they had all gone out except for Nicole and Stella. Kim opened her eyes and looked at them.

"Any better?" Stella asked.

She blinked her eyes yes. "Aspirin," she said,

"helps." She moved her head so she could look directly at Nicole. Nicole looked back at her with large, moist eyes. Suddenly Kim grinned. "Shootout at OK Corral," she said. "Some show."

17

Taps had blown and the camp was quiet, but it felt like a watchful quiet. Stella was sure not many girls were asleep. She had gone down to Point House for a little while and had heard Hen and Johnny explaining the situation to the girls as calmly as if they were discussing a heavy thunderstorm. Eveyone was asked to go directly to her tent after the sing-along and to stay there. If there was a real reason for leaving, "even to go to the loo," Hen said, they should ask a counselor to go along.

"The police will have him by morning, and anyway he's no doubt long gone from this area, but just to be safe," Johnny said.

The girls listened in wide-eyed silence. A few looked alarmed, but there was no panic. Hen played the piano, and the girls sang camp songs for about an hour, and then Hen played some music they could dance to. By the time they left, when Alice blew warning for taps, they all seemed reassured.

Judy, who went with some of the girls and a couple of counselors to the Inn for pre-taps milk and graham crackers, was there when Miss Davenport returned.

She brought the news to Stella, and to Kim, who was back in her own cot. "Poor old Miss D. Here she was coming home triumphant with two canoes she'd gotten cheap in Intervale, driving the truck like an old pro, and what happens? She comes into her own road and she's stopped by like a thousand cops. She had to come up with ID, and she couldn't find her driver's license she was so flustered and scared."

"Oh, poor Miss Davenport," Stella said. "How awful."

"Bet they thought she was the robber in costume," Kim said. "Cops have such fantastic imaginations."

"Well, she was in a state, believe me, by the time she hit the Inn. But Miss Church, our Miss Church, rode to the rescue. She was super. She presented the situation in a nutshell, assured Miss D. there was no problem, and held forth about how wonderful Camp Allegro girls are. It was a real three-handkerchief scene. You could almost hear the violins."

Kim said, "I hope she brought in about how clean our teeth are."

"She persuaded Miss D. that the whole thing is really a public relations plus for the camp."

"Don't send your kid to the fat camp, the French camp, the gymnastics camp," Kim said, "send her to the crime detection camp. Train your kid to be a teen-aged G-girl, prepare her now for the CIA." She yawned. "I won't be able to play tennis for heaven knows how long."

Judy had stayed with Kim while Stella went down to Point House. Now they were all in their beds, and Miss Davenport had made her rounds, saying good night with perhaps a touch more warmth than usual. A light still burned in the Cottage, and when she sat up, Kim could see the shadowy form of Greg, the arts and crafts counselor, sitting with her back to the flagpole. The counselors had set up a surveillance system to last through the night, each of them armed with a whistle. Out on the road, and presumably in other places as well, the police were deployed. The man with the glasses was probably halfway to Canada with his sack of money. She wondered what he had been doing under Point House. Probably had cash stowed away there too. It would be a good place for it, back there in those dusty corners where no one ever looked. After they caught him, she would get Kim to go in there with her, in case some of the money was still there. She thought of the silver dollar that Nicole had found. We should have paid more attention, she thought. It was pretty unlikely, when you stopped to think of it, that some casual tramp would be carrying silver dollars around with him, or would be careless enough to drop one if he did have some. She thought about that man, hiding out around here for almost a year. It must have been a pretty rugged existence. He would have had shelter enough, but how did he keep warm? What did he do about food? She had forgotten to ask Kim if the bag of flour had been opened. Did he make himself pancakes or what? She tried to picture herself as a fugitive for such a long time. It didn't seem as if any amount of money would be worth it, especially if you couldn't spend it. Probably he figured they would give up after a while, and he'd come out from cover. She was pretty sure he was French, maybe French Canadian. He had said, "Me, I kill you dead." She didn't know any French Canadians, but in New Orleans, the French people used that expression. She had been in New Orleans with her parents once for a law convention. Her mother said that use of "me" came from the French habit of saying "*moi*," before the "*je*," for emphasis. She remembered it because she had rather liked it.

She wished she could go to sleep. She was tired. But every little sound caught her attention. Finally she did doze off. When she awoke, it was two thirty by her little alarm clock, and as far as she could tell, everyone in her tent was asleep. She had the feeling that something had awakened her, but she didn't know what it was. She sat up. Greg or someone else was still out by the flagpole, reading with a flashlight. Then the light went off, and the person put her head back, catnapping perhaps.

Stella tensed as the loon screamed. Darned loon. Why did it do that? And for what reason had Nature given that particular bird such an unearthly cry? Swimming the day before, she had seen four smaller dark forms swimming behind the mother loon, and then for a while she had watched as the loon dove and disappeared for what seemed a long time before she reappeared on the surface some distance away. Bringing home the bacon, probably. Bugs for the babies. It was strange how loons could stay under water so long.

She got out of bed quietly and walked to the head of the steps and sat down. It was a beautiful night, cool but not cold, with brilliant starshine. She was going to be sorry to have the summer end. It had turned out about ten thousand times better than she had expected. She thought about Nicole and wondered if she had really changed in the last twenty-four hours, or if the alteration was temporary. Poor Nicole, with a mother like that, no wonder she was obnoxious sometimes. She was glad she had a mom that liked her and that she could talk to.

On the lake beyond the dock, she saw the riding lights of a motorboat, an inboard moving very slowly with a searchlight aimed toward shore. She was sure it was a police boat. There weren't many motorboats down at this end of the lake, especially at night. She hoped they knew the lake. There was a ridge of shallow pebbly bottom for a few feet and then the lake shelved off deeply. A boat could get hung up in the shallow water if the pilot didn't know what he was doing.

She remembered suddenly that she was not supposed to be out of the tent. To her a distance of a few yards would not be "out of," but in Miss Church's mind it probably would be. She started to get up, but she stopped as she saw a canoe drift quietly past, coming from around the bend beyond Point House. It was out a little way, and it carried no lights, but as it came closer she recognized the outlines of Mr. Goldy in the stern and Harry at the bow paddle. They were not drifting, but they were paddling so silently that she could not hear a sound. She wished she could paddle that well. They were like Indians, moving along toward the dock area. It was comforting to know that Mr. Goldy and Harry were out there. She wondered where Herbert was. Maybe he'd run off with the money he had scooped up at Moore's Pond.

In a few minutes the canoe had circled and was retracing its route, a little farther out in the lake this time, past Point House and out of sight. Probably they went as far as the men's tent, around the bend in the lake, and then turned back. She yawned. Might as well go back to bed.

She stood up. Behind her under the flagpole she could see that Greg was slumped back against the pole, asleep. Good thing she's not in the Army, she thought; they shoot people for falling asleep on watch. She had her back to Point House now, one foot on the step above her, but something made her turn around, some slight difference in the sleepy sound of the water lapping against the shore. She looked back. A rowboat keeping very close to shore was beaching under Point House. She could see the faint white A on the bow that indicated it was an Allegro boat. Another counselor checking up, no doubt. She stepped back into the shadows, curious to know who it was but not wanting to be caught out of her tent.

A figure stepped out of the boat and tied it loosely to one of the pilings that supported Point House. It was too dark to see who it was. The person looked around in a stealthy kind of way that suddenly alerted her. She moved down the steps a little way so she could keep him or her in sight. It was someone with long hair, she could tell by the silhouette. Then whoever it was moved out of sight, and she heard the faint creak of the wood slats. She held her breath. In a couple of minutes the figure came out carrying something. It looked like a sack.

Mr. Goldy's canoe had just come into sight again, some distance out, moving like a shadow through the water. The person below her saw it at the same moment that she did. He shrank back into the shadows and waited. When the canoe had gone by, he moved toward the boat, hoisting the sack on his shoulder. He glanced up at the Point House steps and Stella saw the glint of his glasses.

18

For a moment she stood perfectly still, sure that he could see her. Then she began to unfreeze a little. He had not seen her. At the moment that she had caught the gleam of his spectacles, he had been standing in an open space with his face lifted upward. Trapped by starlight, she thought, and had a wild impulse to giggle. He did not seem to have his gun in his hand. No doubt it was in the boat. If he left while Mr. Goldy was up at the dock end, he could go downlake, around the Point, keeping close to shore, and possibly not be seen by anyone. That end of the lake went on for nearly a mile, and if he rowed to the end, he might actually get clear away.

All this flashed through her mind while the man still stood there. Then he put one foot on the gunwale of the boat. Stella placed her little fingers in the corners of her mouth and gave out an ear-splitting whistle. Instantly things began to happen. Other whistles blew all over camp. Mr. Goldy's canoe reappeared, and the searchlight on the police boat swung around toward Point House as the boat changed course.

The man, still carrying the sack, made several false starts, once as if to get into the boat, then as if to dart off into the scrub. But as the canoe and the police boat approached, he ran up onto Point House deck and along it toward the far, dark end. She heard Mr. Goldy yell, "Hold it!" And then a voice came through a megaphone. "Freeze right where you are. Empty your hands."

The man had moved out of her sight. Behind her she heard voices, low-pitched and anxious, as the camp began to gather. She heard Johnny say, "Keep back. Keep back." And then Miss Davenport, sounding very calm, saying, "It will be all right. They have him now."

"Look!" It was Nicole's voice. "He's on the railing."

Stella saw him standing where the two sides of the deck met at the far end. He was poised on the railing, still holding the sack. The police searchlight caught him and pinned him in light. The voice with the megaphone gave him orders. "Stay where you are. Throw down what you're holding. Put up your hands."

She heard Hen's low voice just behind her. "He's going to jump."

They held their breath. For a second he swayed in a kind of crouch. Then he jumped into the lake, not a dive but a huddled-up jump with his knees up, like a kid taking his first leap into the lake. They heard the splash. No one spoke. Then someone pushed past Stella down the stairs so she could see better, and all of them began to move down. They weren't shoving, but they wanted to see, and the words the counselors and Miss Davenport were saying were not even heard.

Stella was propelled along by the crowd behind her. She wished Kim were there. If anyone ought to be in the finish, it was Kim. At the bottom of the steps they spilled out onto the deck and down onto the narrow strip of beach. Stella leaned over the porch rail. She could see people in the police boat hauling the man out of the water. He was limp. Mr. Goldy's canoe was holding alongside the police boat. Harry leaned over toward the water with his flashlight.

"Look!" It was Eva Lynde, close behind Stella, speaking in an awed voice. "Pieces of paper all over the water. All over! It's money!"

Hundreds of bills floated around the boat, some of them drifting away in the pull of the waves. Harry scooped up a handful and held them up. A man on the police boat leaned over with a fishnet and began to gather up some of the bills. They were getting wet and beginning to sink.

A girl's voice said, "I'm going to get me some of that," and there was a surge toward the steps, but Miss Davenport stood there, looking very formidable.

"No!" she said in a voice that carried. "Any girl who touches any of that money will be reported to the police for obstructing justice."

That stopped them.

"Shoot," somebody said. "I could have bought me a ten-speed bike."

"That's stolen money, dummy," Hen said. "It belongs to the bank, whatever they can get their hands on."

The man with the megaphone spoke to them, his voice suddenly booming out of the dark and startling them. "All clear. Thank you very much." Someone started up the engine, and the boat took off fast toward the village.

Miss Davenport went down to the shore and waited for Mr. Goldy and Herbert to come in close enough to speak to. In a few minutes she came back and faced the campers. She seemed very calm and in charge.

"They have captured the bank robber," she said. "He is identified as the robber."

Nicole's voice called out. "Is he dead?"

"No, but he is badly hurt. He jumped into shallow water."

Somebody said, "Ouch!"

"The police will be back in the morning to retrieve as much of the money as possible. No one is to go near the lake until that is done. You understand that. No one is to go near the lake. You would be interfering with evidence. The scene of the crime must be left untouched."

"Gotta get them fingerprints," a familiar voice murmured just behind Stella. She turned and saw Kim standing on one leg, clinging to the railing.

"You have all behaved well," Miss Davenport said. "Now go to bed and pleasant dreams."

Stella helped Kim hop back up the steps, stopping

on every step to wait for the pain to subside. Hen saw them and helped.

"You shouldn't be here," she said.

"You think I was going to miss the last act curtain?"

They helped her into her tent, and Miss Church brought her a glass of water and some aspirin.

"Well," Miss Church said, "that's that."

"I'll never forget the sight of all that wet money," Judy said.

"Drowning in his own greed," Miss Church said. "Hoist by his own petard. Just like *The Treasure of the Sierra Madre*."

"Miss Church, you see too many movies," Kim said.

"Go to sleep now. Have you brushed your teeth?"

"Twice," Kim said.

"Dream about butterflies," said Miss Church.

19

It was an important assembly and even Kim was there, her leg encased in the wide bandage that the doctor at the hospital had put on. Miss Davenport had not told them what was special about this assembly, but there was a strange man sitting beside her as she rose to greet the campers.

"First," she said, "a few loose ends of news. The man, Jacques Burdine, a native of Nova Scotia, has confessed to the robbery last fall of the bank in Center Ossipee. The man is still in the hospital in critical condition. Secondly, our young friend Herbert has returned the money he took from Moore's Pond, and also he has confessed to ringing the bell on that mysterious occasion. He thought, and I quote, It would be a blast, unquote."

The campers laughed.

"I might add that Herbert isn't with us any more."

Stella stole a glance at Nicole and saw that she was laughing with the rest, as if Herbert meant nothing at all to her.

"Mr. Burdine has confessed that it was he who

threw rocks at Stella, out on the hill past the Inn. The place where she liked to go and sit was near one of the spots where he had, I think the word is, 'stashed' some of his 'loot.' He wanted to frighten her away from there. You see, he had a very cozy hideout here, all last year, but then suddenly workmen arrived, and he had no chance to dig up all of his money, which he had buried securely in several different places. We had workers here seven days a week, working until dark every day, to get the camp ready in time. Some of the money he did manage to move over to Moore's Pond, where he felt safe until the girls began intruding there too. He thought of going away, but that was risky with no plan worked out, and he decided that if he could hold out until we left, he would have his comfortable home-away-from-home for the winter. By next spring it might be safe to leave and go to Canada, or so he told the police. I might add that not having talked to anyone for more than a year, he seemed unable to stop talking once he started.

"It was he who stole the bag of flour, and apparently other food as well, before Herbert put the lock on the supply room.

"It was he who was under Point House, trying to get out the money that was there. And I must apologize to Stella for having insisted it was only an animal she saw.

"You have seen the money floating tantalizingly on the lake. The police have retrieved a good deal of it, sodden but negotiable, and also the money at Moore's

Pond, and in a small cave near where Stella was stoned. Some of that had apparently been already removed, but a few bills remained. As Kim suspected, there was a good deal hidden under the old boat at Moore's Pond, where, I feel I must add, she should *not* have been exploring."

Nicole looked quickly at Kim.

"I am proud of the poise and control of all of you during this trying time, and I especially commend Stella and Kim and Nicole and our swimming counselor Hen Norton for conspicuous bravery under fire, as it were. I should like to also commend Hen and Johnny and Miss Church for their superb handling of a dangerous situation during my unfortunate absence. I like to think that you all performed in the Allegro tradition." She waited for the smattering of applause to die down. "And now this morning I am happy to introduce to you the president of the Center Ossipee Bank, Mr. Gordon Chase." She turned toward the white-haired man and bowed. "Mr. Chase."

Mr. Chase acknowledged their applause and smiled. "Thank you, Miss Davenport, and Allegro campers. And that is not an idle thank you. I have come here this morning to try to tell you how grateful I am, my bank is, for the recovery of a large sum of money that we thought had disappeared forever. I must agree with Miss Davenport that you all behaved in an exemplary manner. I am glad to discover for myself that all those stories I have been hearing and reading about our selfish, undisciplined youth are poppycock."

Somebody said, "Hear-hear," and everyone laughed and clapped.

"I am here this morning not only to thank you, but to tell you that there was a reward for the recovery of the stolen money, and pursuant to the instructions accompanying the offer of the reward, I am happy to present to Camp Allegro a cashier's check for ten thousand dollars." He turned and held out the check to Miss Davenport, who was obviously taken by surprise.

She gasped and put her hand to her mouth. Then she stood up and accepted the check, and for a moment she was too moved to speak. "I had no idea," she said. "I had no idea. Oh, girls, now we can put a new roof on Point House! We can buy a new pickup truck next year."

"And two new canoes," Hen said.

Miss Davenport thanked Mr. Chase repeatedly, and the music counselor leaped to the occasion by conducting a song for Mr. Chase, an old camp greeting. "How do you do, Mr. Chase, how do you do, Is there anything that we can do for you? We will do the best we can and we'll treat you like a man, How do you do, Mr. Chase, how do you do-oo-oo."

"Honestly," Kim said, hobbling out of Point House on her new cane made for her by Mr. Goldy, "honestly, somebody ought to do something about the words of camp songs. I mean 'and we'll treat you like a man'! Really!"

"Oh, well," Stella said. "Next year you can write some brilliant new ones."

"Do you think Miss D. would take us on as junior counselors in a couple or three years?"

"We can ask. I think you have to be sixteen."

"Mr. Goldy said he'd like to have me as assistant tennis counselor."

"What would I do? I'm not outstanding at anything."

"You could be in charge of the 'Racket.'"

They passed a small group of girls who were clustered around Nicole. Nicole, whose back was toward Stella and Kim, was holding forth. "Well, I just told him, I said, 'You put that gun down,' I said. 'If you kill me, you'll get the chair, and you'll have to kill me if you shoot that gun at my friend again.'"

Someone said, "Oh, Nicole, weren't you scared?"

"Of course. But I did what I had to do." She turned her head and saw Kim and Stella, then turned away again quickly as if she had not seen them, and said in a louder voice, "Kim was terrific. Kim was so brave, you wouldn't believe."

Stella and Kim went on up the steps. "Honestly," Stella said. "I suppose she'll live on that drama for the next five years. Nicole Nasby in a thrilling adventure story entitled, 'Snatching My Best Friend from the Jaws of Death.'"

Kim laughed. "Oh, well," she said, "she's entitled."